Susan Carlisle's love affair with books began in the sixth grade, when she made a bad grade in mathematics. Not allowed to watch TV until she'd brought the grade up, Susan filled her time with books. She turned her love of reading into a passion for writing, and now has over ten Medical Romances published through Mills & Boon. She writes about hot, sexy docs and the strong women who captivate them. Visit SusanCarlisle.com.

Also by Susan Carlisle

The Doctor's Redemption
His Best Friend's Baby
One Night Before Christmas
Married for the Boss's Baby
White Wedding for a Southern Belle
The Doctor's Sleigh Bell Proposal
The Surgeon's Cinderella

Heart of Mississippi miniseries

The Doctor Who Made Her Love Again
The Maverick Who Ruled Her Heart

Discover more at millsandboon.co.uk.

STOLEN KISSES WITH HER BOSS

BY
SUSAN CARLISLE

MILLS & BOON

This is a work of fiction. Names, characters, places, locations and incidents are purely fictional and bear no relationship to any real life individuals, living or dead, or to any actual places, business establishments, locations, events or incidents. Any resemblance is entirely coincidental.

First published in Great Britain 2017
by Mills & Boon, an imprint of HarperCollins*Publishers*
1 London Bridge Street, London, SE1 9GF

Large Print edition 2018

ISBN: 978-0-263-07256-3

This book is produced from independently certified FSC™ paper to ensure responsible forest management. For more information visit www.harpercollins.co.uk/green.

Printed and bound in Great Britain
by CPI Group (UK) Ltd, Croydon, CR0 4YY

To Anastasia Huff.
Thanks for all your love and support.

CHAPTER ONE

CYNTHIA MARCUM TAPPED the mouse of her laptop. Her emails came into view. Scanning them, she paused when she saw one from Dr. Sean Donavon. Her body tingled in anticipation. Why would he be emailing her? Her interactions had always been with his staff. Had she done something wrong?

She had been doing Dr. Donavon's transcription for just over a month now. He was an otolaryngologist and one of five surgeons she typed dictation for in the metropolitan Birmingham, Alabama area. The pay was so good she'd added him to her client list despite already having a full load. She could use the money. Her brothers, Mark and Rick, were always in need of something costing at least a hundred dollars.

The money wasn't the only thing she enjoyed about working for the mystery doctor. She loved the sound of his voice. It drew her in. She always saved his tapes for last. His deep resonating tone was smooth and silky like warm chocolate. It brought to mind a cool night with rain tapping against a tin roof and him pulling her close.

Her imagination worked overtime where Dr. Donavon was concerned. She couldn't get enough of listening to him, often playing his tapes back more than once. Even all the medical terms sounded erotic when he uttered them.

She often wondered if he looked like he sounded. All dark and sexy.

A *humph* escaped her. Yeah, more like short and bald. That had happened one time when she had met a radio DJ. Based on his voice she'd built him up into this young, buff guy who every woman would want. Unfortunately, he turned out to be a short, middle-aged man with a gray ponytail. To say she had been disappointed was an understatement.

Listening to Dr. Donavon had become her romantic outlet. Since she currently had no one special in her life, hearing his voice had filled that void. She'd been in a relationship when her parents died. Wedding bells with Dave hadn't seemed too far off, then life had happened. Her parents' estate issues, the needs of her brothers and everything in between had worked against their relationship.

Dave had soon begun complaining that she wasn't spending enough time with him. It had then gone into, "I didn't sign on to help raise two teenage boys." Finally, he'd told her he had found someone else. In a way Cynthia was relieved. He just didn't share her mind-set about the importance of family. He didn't understand her or the necessity of keeping her family together at all costs.

After they broke up, she didn't try to have another solid relationship. She'd dated a few times but never let the guys close enough to matter. Usually, when they found out she was responsible for her brothers, they quickly backed away. Now wasn't the time for a man and she'd accepted that. Sadly, until the boys were more settled in life she would just have to get her thrills from listening to Dr. Donavon. And he was well worth listening to.

Her finger hovered over the computer mouse. Would his emails be just as amazing? Yeah right. She'd been without a man far too long when fantasy started overtaking reality. She clicked the email, opening it.

Then she read the black words against the white screen.

Hello, Ms. Marcum,
My office manager gave me your name as the person who has been preparing my transcriptions. I'm very impressed with your work.

The reason I'm contacting you is that I am currently in the middle of putting together a grant proposal and need to have some extra reports transcribed over the next few weeks. I wanted to know if you would be willing to take on this additional work. Of course I will compensate you for your time.

I would really appreciate your help.
Regards,
S. Donavon

Nope. Nothing sexy there. But he sounded nice. Considerate. In her mind she could almost hear him say the words. Cynthia reread the message. There wasn't much time in her days. Taking on more work might be difficult. This was Rick's senior year in high school so what extra hours she had were spent going to his activities. Yet the extra money Dr. Donavon offered would help pay for Mark's college tuition that was due soon.

Plus, she liked to keep her clients happy. Took pride in her work. So far that hadn't been a problem with any of her employers. And she would get to listen to his voice more often. But if she didn't agree to Dr. Donavon's request would he take all his work elsewhere? She couldn't afford to let that happen.

Moving the cursor to the reply button, she clicked and typed.

Dr. Donavon,
I'm glad you're pleased with my work. My time is tight at present, but I'll do my best to fit in any extra reports you send.

I don't know how quick a turnaround time I can promise, but I will make it as short as possible.
Cynthia

Scanning the message, she made sure she had used the correct tone, then clicked "send". She didn't want to lose his business but couldn't overextend herself either. Her brothers, her family, took priority—always. The upside was if there was enough money from the extra work maybe she could start looking for a new car. Hers was on its last legs. She grinned. More like last tire.

Since she had left nursing school to become a full-time transcriptionist she'd gained a reputation as being competent and professional. It had been difficult to build a client list. She'd been tickled to add Dr. Donavon. As a surgeon, he produced plenty of work to keep her busy. He also paid better than her other clients. Getting to enjoy his voice almost daily was an added perk.

"Hey, Cyn," Rick called. His tall, lanky body appeared in the doorway of the small front room of their house she used as an office. He wore his usual uniform of jeans and well-worn T-shirt. "I'm going over to Joey's house."

Cynthia swiveled in the chair to face him. "Do you have that project done?"

"Almost." He put up a hand stopping her from saying more. "I'll have it finished tomorrow and it isn't due for another week. Don't worry, I have all A's."

"Yeah, but you don't want that to slip. That scholarship you're after depends on it."

Rick waved a hand at her. "You worry too much. See ya."

Seconds later the back door squeaked open and slammed closed.

She did worry. That had been her full-time job since her parents had died in that devastating car accident. She'd become guardian of her brothers when she was only a few years older. It hadn't been easy for any of them but they were making it.

Her father had told her more than once, "Cynthia, family is everything. You have to support your family." She lived by that motto. She would honor her parents by seeing that her brothers had a good start in the world. Once they were settled, she would go back to school and think about her own future. She missed that carefree time when she'd been on her own. The times she hadn't had to consider her brothers before she did something as simple as go out for the night.

The three of them had inherited the house, but there were still day-to-day expenses to meet. Those came out of her paycheck. Her parents had left some money but it wouldn't last long if she tapped into it. What her parents had left them was for the boys' higher education or to help them buy their own place.

Enough pondering. She had work to finish. Glancing at her email list one last time, she saw that there was a new note from Dr. Donavon. She opened it.

I can't say thank you enough.

I'll send over the dictation electronically this afternoon and will need the reports by Monday morning. Is that doable? If you can get them done by then I'll owe you big-time.

S. Donavon

She could imagine the smile on his face when he read her email. She liked it that she'd made him happy. But work so soon? This weekend? He really must be in a hurry. Well, she knew what her plans were for tonight and tomorrow morning.

Dr. Donavon,

I'll do my best to have them ready by Monday.

Cynthia

Seconds later he came back.

You're a lifesaver.
S. Donavon

Cynthia wasn't sure she could be anyone else's lifesaver. She was already taking care of more people than she could manage now. Taking on someone else might sink her boat. What would it be like to have someone take care of her for a change?

The kitchen door opened and slammed shut. "Cyn?" Mark, who was just three years younger than her, called.

"In here."

He flopped into the cushion chair beside her desk and flung a leg over the arm.

"So how did it go today?" Cynthia asked.

"I'm going to quit."

His blunt statement wasn't unexpected. She leaned toward him, gripping the arms of her chair. Her parents had wanted them all to get a college education. She'd been fighting Mark's apathy about doing that for months now. The weight of doing so was starting to get to her. "Why?"

"College doesn't get you anywhere." Mark spoke to the floor instead of her.

This was one of those times when she wished she had some backup, someone to turn to. She refused to let her voice rise. “You know Mom and Dad wouldn’t like that.”

“Yeah. But it’s not for me.”

Cynthia moved the chair to face him more directly. “Then what’re you going to do?”

He shrugged and continued to look at that floor. “I don’t know.”

That wasn’t a good plan. “Well, you’re going to have to figure something out.”

Mark jumped to his feet. “Get off my back. You’re not my parent. We can’t all be Rick.” He stomped from the room.

She sighed. Could the day get any better? Mark’s statement hurt on a number of levels. Cynthia missed her parents too. That was why she took her guardianship responsibilities seriously. Wanted to do the best by them. And no, she was not Mark’s parent. If the situation was different she would prefer just being his sister.

Dr. Donavon’s dictation arrived in her transcription system’s inbox right before dinner. The work could wait until after dinner. Her parents had made the evening meal time important and she continued the practice. Her brothers knew that if possible they were expected at home at six during the week so they could spend some time together.

Two hours later she pulled her chair up to her desk. This wasn't the way she'd planned to spend Friday night, but she would get over it. Doing what had to be done had become a part of her life. She'd have Dr. Donavon's work to him Monday morning, hoping to impress.

She clicked the dictation inbox and Dr. Donavon's voice filled her ears. It didn't take long for her to forget about how tired she was or the amount of housework that needed doing and start enjoying the rich deepness of his voice. If she had to work on Friday night, there were worse jobs to have than one that involved having the sound of a sexy voice in her ear.

After lunch Monday, Sean settled in behind his desk at his clinic office. Pushing his chair back and putting his feet on his desk, he crossed his ankles and got comfortable. He didn't usually reread all his reports but in this instance, he couldn't afford not to. The grant was too important.

His future depended on it. Not to mention the quality of life for his patients, for the vast number of patients who would have their hearing improved and those of other ear, nose and throat doctors as well. With the grant he could continue his research and make that difference.

With the success of his procedure and the patent of a new instrument he would also be financially set for life. He knew too well what it was like being without and he'd vowed never to feel that way again. He'd heard some people call it the Scarlett O'Hara syndrome. He just called it smart.

Long ago he'd hired a financial planner. He was determined not to live paycheck to paycheck as his parents had, wondering if there would be enough cash to pay the bills or buy food. While growing up, more than once he'd been unable to participate with his friends in an activity because there hadn't been funds. His parents had been and still were the types to fall in with the next big money-making scheme, which always cost them money instead of making them rich as they claimed they one day would be. There had been multi-level marketing, investing in commercial ventures or selling the next great vitamin product. Nothing seemed to work but they were always in for the chance it might.

Sean hated any part of that way of life. Money shouldn't be squandered. Instead it should be saved and invested. He was determined to do just that. Their attitude toward paying their bills and handling finances embarrassed him. Their philosophy about life was so different from his that they found little in common. Because of that he'd not seen them in almost a year. Even then visits had been short. He wasn't interested in hearing about the next "get rich quick" plan.

The one thing about his new breakthrough was that it would allow him to put away enough money to support his parents in their old age. He was confident that they would need his help. Despite his bitter feelings about his childhood he would take care of them. No matter what, they were his parents.

Now he only had to get the grant documentation in order. The submission must be flawless. The competition was tight, right down to the written documents. Even the smallest element could make a difference between him and someone else receiving the grant.

Picking up his tablet, he pulled up his most recent reports and started reading. Halfway through the first one, he was pleased to find not a single mistake. Not that he really expected one but he couldn't be too careful. Ms. Marcum had done a superb job and certainly in a timely manner. He should tell her so.

When his last transcriptionist had taken another position she'd given his office manager Ms. Marcum's name along with a glowing reference. Because he didn't have time to waste completing the grant he'd told his office manager to hire her without further question. Not known for making snap decisions, thankfully this one had been a smart one. He didn't know what would have happened to his grant submission if she hadn't been willing to take on the additional work.

Now he needed to make sure he kept her. He couldn't have her quitting just when he needed her the most. He didn't have time to waste hiring another, especially when there was no guarantee that the next person would be any good. His manager had already said they were lucky to get this one. He needed his dictation done in a timely manner and she had proven she could do that.

Pulling up his email, he entered Cynthia Marcum's address. Her name made her sound like a middle-aged matron. It didn't matter what she looked like. What concerned him was the quality of his papers and keeping her typing them.

Ms. Marcum,
I have reviewed your reports and I'm very pleased with your work. Thank you for getting them to me in such a timely manner. I was pleasantly surprised to learn that they were waiting for me when I returned to my office after coming out of surgery today.

I can't say enough about how much I appreciate your efforts. I hope it's still okay to send you additional work.
Very gratefully,
S. Marcum

Without hesitation he clicked the "send" button.

* * *

Cynthia was pleased to have his gratitude. It was always nice to get affirmation for her efforts. Good manners and a sexy voice. Two for two as far as she was concerned.

As much as she liked his praise she didn't want to have to stay up late or work on weekends to get it. Hopefully other work he sent wouldn't require her doing so. She'd handle that issue when the time came, if it did. She also had to honor her other clients' needs as well.

Cynthia typed a message.

Dr. Donavon,
I'm so happy you were pleased. Just let me know if I can help out further.
Cynthia

She reread the note twice. It was polite, yet businesslike.

A minute later a message landed in her mailbox.

Thank you! I do, in fact, have more work for you. I will send it through today.
S. Donavon

Maybe she'd offered too quickly. Apparently this grant was extremely important to him. At least he hadn't put a time period on when he needed these reports returned.

In the middle of the afternoon the doorbell rang. Cynthia answered it to find a delivery man holding a green plant in a blue ceramic pot.

"Cynthia Marcum?"

"Yes."

"This is for you." The man handed her the pot.

Dumbfounded, Cynthia was left to stare at it as he climbed into his van. No one had ever sent her something from a florist. There had been flower arrangements when her parents died but never something just for her. What was going on?

She looked down at the full, beautiful plant with broad leaves and a vivid red flower in the center. Tucked under one of the leaves was a white envelope with her name scrawled on it. Closing the door with her foot, she carried the plant to her office and set it on the corner of her desk. Removing the envelope, she pulled out the card inside. Written on it was: "Thanks, Sean Donavon."

He'd sent her a thank-you plant. Cynthia

couldn't help but smile. That was thoughtful. Dr. Donavon had just earned another point. No matter what he looked like she could fall for someone who took the time to say thank you. She loved her brothers but "thank you" wasn't something she regularly heard. She didn't regret her sacrifices or what she did for them but she would like some understanding and appreciation sometimes. She looked at the plant again. Dr. Donavon's office manager had no doubt taken care of sending the gift.

A short time later the work he wanted done came up in her system.

She opened her email and clicked "compose."

Dr. Donavon
Thank you so much for the beautiful plant. You shouldn't have, but I will enjoy having it on my desk.
I received your dictation and will work on it today and tomorrow. I'll send the reports when they are completed.
Cynthia

It was almost midnight on Tuesday when she finally finished the last of her work. She'd spent most of the early part of her day typing her other clients' dictation. Rick had had a basketball game that evening and that had meant she'd made it back to her desk chair late. Still she was determined to have all her typing done so she could start fresh the next day. That meant working late.

Wednesday morning, she opened Dr. Donavon's normal surgical dictation and listened for the soft cadence of his voice as he spoke through her headphones. Smiling, she reached out and touched the tip of one leaf on her plant. Between his usual work and the special assignment, she was getting to spend many hours with his delicious voice. She was becoming moony-eyed over a man she'd never seen and knew nothing about. He could be married for all she knew. Enough of that—she needed to get to work.

Hours later she punched a key and sent the twenty separate reports she'd finished off to his electronic folder.

Feeling good about what she had accomplished that day, she took a long, hot shower before heading to bed. Having forgotten to turn off the kitchen light, she headed down the hallway. As she passed her office door she noticed the light flashing on her cell phone, indicating she had an email waiting. She received few this time of night so she feared it might be something important. It was from Dr. Donavon.

Had she tried she couldn't have slowed her rapid heartbeat. What was he doing working this late? She should wait until morning to open it but it would mean she would stay awake wondering what he had to say. Far too eager for her comfort, she double-tapped the key.

Thank you for the reports and you're welcome for the plant. It was just my small way of saying thank you.
Good night.
S. Donavon

How could a simple business email make her so giddy? She had to get a grip where Dr. Donavon was concerned. More than his voice was starting to get to her. What would it sound like to have him say good night in her ear? A shiver went up her spine. Cynthia shook her head. She'd been up too late. Her mind was beginning to play tricks on her.

She climbed into bed, pulled her quilt over her and smiled before drifting off to sleep.

Sean didn't make a practice of sending someone a thank-you gift for helping him with work he was already paying them to do, but he liked Ms. Marcum.

She'd really helped him out. He'd never sent a plant, or flowers for that matter, before. Even after a date. As far as he was concerned they were a waste of money, which was better used on something practical like a power bill or making an investment.

From the tone of Ms. Marcum's emails, she seemed an agreeable person. Someone he could work well with for a long time. Sean liked to keep good employees happy to prevent having to search for new ones. He'd been successful at it too. His office manager and several of his nurses had been with him for years.

He wasn't in the habit of taking chances. He'd seen more than once growing up what happened when someone took a chance. He didn't do it with places to live, friends or when making decisions on which stocks to buy. Only sure things interested him. That was just what the grant proposal had to be: a sure thing. Ms. Marcum was going to help make that happen.

Sean had worked until two o'clock in the morning the night before and still hadn't gone through all the reports and information he needed to review. Organization wasn't his strongest skill. He was going to need help. He moved a pile of disordered papers to another area of his desk, then more to another spot.

Disorganization was one trait he'd gotten from his parents that he couldn't seem to shake. It was almost ingrained. When they got involved in one of their schemes, record-keeping was part of the process and they didn't do it well. Soon they had no idea how deep they were in financially and couldn't put their hands on the documentation to figure it out.

When his father discovered the severity of it he would go out and get an hourly job. Then when the next big moneymaker scam came along his father would quit his job and devote all his time to building the new "business." Sean had heard all his life, "This will be it. We'll be on the road to riches this time." That time had yet to come.

He'd left all he could of that behind, except for being unorganized. He needed someone good with written documentation computer skills to assist him. The sooner the better. He only had a few weeks until the submission must be flawless.

Ms. Marcum had done another superb job with the latest reports. She seemed efficient. In her last email she'd offered her assistance. Would she consider helping him out for a few weeks? There was only one way to find out.

Ms. Marcum, I have a proposition for you.

Sean chuckled. Maybe those weren't the correct words.

Ms. Marcum, would you be able to come by my office around three p.m. tomorrow? I have an opportunity that I would like to discuss with you in person.
S. Donavon

Hopefully she would agree to their meeting and his need for help. He couldn't allow her to refuse him. How was he going to get the work done if she didn't assist him? His office staff was already busy enough. There was no time to hire someone else to handle it. He was reaching desperation level. Somehow he must gain her cooperation.

CHAPTER TWO

IT WAS LATE in the morning when Cynthia opened the email she'd saved for last.

She responded.

I'm sorry but I have another appointment at three. Can we make it four?

After a moment's hesitation she sent the email out. She was tempted to rearrange her entire afternoon. She really needed this job. But Rick's meeting with the scholarship council was too important to miss.

She didn't have to wait long for a reply.

I have rounds at four. How about we make it five?
I won't keep you long, I promise.
S. Donavon.

Seconds later she typed: See you at five.

That afternoon Cynthia entered the glass doors of a modern single-story brick building. It was located across the street from the large multi-story hospital in the center of Birmingham. A free-standing sign indicated the building contained Dr. Donavon's office. It was late in the day and only a few cars occupied the parking lot. Most of the patients would have been seen and the staff was probably leaving for the day.

She'd only been here one other time when she'd signed her employment papers. Transcribers worked behind the scenes and Cynthia liked it that way. She didn't have to leave home and that suited her lifestyle perfectly. That way she was able to work her schedule around her brothers' needs. It was highly unusual for a doctor to call her to his office. So why was Dr. Donavon doing so now?

Doctors' pictures were usually posted on their websites but she'd made it a point not to look for Dr. Donavon's because she didn't want to ruin her fantasy image of him. His appearance didn't matter anyway; this certainly wasn't a social call.

With a flutter of trepidation in her belly, she stepped to the reception window. Would she be disappointed when she saw him? The young woman with platinum blond hair and bright red fingernails behind the glass looked at her. She asked with an edge to her voice, "May I help you?"

"I'm here to see Dr. Donavon," Cynthia said in a firm tone.

The woman looked down her nose at her as if Cynthia had requested the impossible. "Is he expecting you?"

"Yes. I'm Cynthia Marcum. The transcriptionist. He told me to be here at five."

"Let me see if he's still here." She picked up the phone and spoke to the person on the other end. Putting it down, she said briskly, "He'll be right out. Just have a seat."

Cynthia did as she suggested. She studied the functional room containing metal chairs and a few end tables. There was a magazine rack on the wall and a fake potted plant in the corner. It was quiet and there was only a lone overhead light on. Minutes later the woman switched off the lights over her desk, came out from behind it and headed out of the front door without a glance in Cynthia's direction.

Was she alone in the building with just Dr.

Donavon? What did she really know about the man? Even doctors could be ax murderers. She should have said no to meeting him after-hours. Waited until morning. She hoped she was a good judge of character even if her decision was based on emails alone. Shaking the idea off, she nervously shifted in her chair. She'd been so caught up in her fantasy she hadn't been thinking straight. Now she was letting her nerves get the better of her. Surely there was someone else in the office as well.

Cynthia watched the minute hand move for five agonizingly slow minutes before sounds of footsteps coming in her direction caught her attention.

What did he look like? The flutter increased, along with her curiosity. Steps grew closer. The quivering grew to a swirling. She felt as if she were going to meet her favorite rock star. After the way she'd pictured him maybe she was.

Cynthia shook her head and glanced at the ceiling to regain rational thought. She stood. No one could be that good-looking no matter how wonderful his voice was.

She was wrong. On both counts. The man towering over her was at least six feet tall. With dark hair and crystal-blue eyes, he would make any woman swoon. The fact he still wore a white lab coat over a blue-checked button-down shirt and tan pants didn't hurt his look of authority. He was glossy-magazine-front-cover gorgeous!

Her breath caught as she stared. His looks matched his voice and then some. And she was making a fool of herself right in front of him.

He smiled while giving her an odd look. "Ms. Marcum?"

Cynthia let out the breath she'd been holding. When had she ever been so focused on someone's looks? She wasn't that shallow. Still this man had her gaping at him. She needed to find a flaw if she was going to regain her sanity. She croaked, "Yes." Then cleared her throat and continued. "Please call me Cynthia. I'm not much on formal names."

"Good. Come with me. We can talk in my office."

He started down the hall. When she didn't follow immediately he stopped and looked at her. "Ms. Marcum. Cynthia?"

"I'm sorry. I'm coming." She needed to get control. Stop embarrassing herself.

She followed him along a hall with exam rooms on both sides. She saw a nurse standing at a counter at the end of the hall. With relief, she saw they weren't alone after all.

He stood beside an open doorway, inviting her to enter by extending a hand. He joined her, making the area suddenly feel small. Moving behind a desk that had seen better days and was piled high with paper stacks, he remained on his feet. Positioned on her side of the desk was a straight-backed wooden chair that reminded her of one in the library of her elementary school and appeared just as inviting.

"It's so nice to meet you, Cynthia. Please have a seat." He took the chair on squeaky wheels behind his desk. It was by no means the latest model either.

Cynthia sat, then glanced around. This might be the saddest doctor's office she'd ever seen. She'd envisioned a businesslike area filled with books, which this one was, but it also had a feeling of neglect. Somehow she had expected more. Minimal yes, but not so outdated and drab.

There were no pictures of a wife or children, not even a dog. No indication of a hobby. No curtains hung above the utilitarian blinds. The one lone lamp on the desk only added to the sadness of the cluttered atmosphere. The space was an enormous contrast to the outstandingly handsome man sitting in front of her. What had happened to him for him to keep his personal space so…impersonal?

Did his home look this needy as well? Didn't he have a wife, a mother, or at least a girlfriend who could help him out with decorating? Every fiber in her wanted to buy him an antique desk and two tufted chairs. He needed her plant worse than she did.

Dr. Donavon cleared his throat and her attention returned to him. Those piercing blue eyes watched her closely. "You don't like my office?"

He was observant. She needed to make sure she schooled her emotions from showing too much on her face. "I just hadn't expected your office to look…um…like this. Sometimes I let my imagination carry me away."

Dr. Donavon leaned back in his chair giving

her a direct look with a small smile on his lips. "How's that?"

She glanced around again. "I don't know. I just thought it might not be so uh…" How could she say this without sounding critical? "Maybe have more chrome and glass."

"I'm not really into chrome and glass."

Cynthia gave a nervous laugh. "I'm not either. Please forget I said anything. You didn't ask me here to insult your décor or to be your interior decorator."

"My apologies as well. I didn't mean to put you on the spot. You're not what I expected either."

"I hope you aren't disappointed." She wasn't sure where this meeting was going.

"I would say quite to the contrary. You're a pleasant surprise." He continued to study her.

Cynthia didn't know how to react to that statement. What had he expected? Was he flirting with her? It had been so long since a man had, she wasn't sure she would recognize it when it happened. "Thank you, I think."

"It was a compliment. I'm being rude and have embarrassed you. That's certainly not what I intended, especially when I need to ask you a favor."

"Ask me? A f-favor?" she stammered.

"Yes. I'd like you to consider helping me get the final draft of my grant proposal together." He gave her a charming smile. "I could really use your help." He made a point of indicating the stacks on his desk.

"Me? Why me? I don't know anything about putting together a grant."

"Maybe not, but I can help with that. From what I can tell you have good organizational skills on the computer and you're a fast and accurate typist. I need those skills to get this grant out on time. If you'll accept my proposition, I'll pay you time and half."

Heat crept up the back of her neck. She was sure he hadn't realized what he'd said about a proposition but she had. After fantasizing about him, and now seeing that he was devastatingly attractive, her mind was coming up with crazy ideas. Cynthia shifted in her seat. She must be careful not to make a fool of herself. "I've already agreed to do your transcription."

"Yes, but I need someone who can help me get

my grant reports in order. Put the documents into the format and order required ASAP."

"I appreciate your offer. But I'm going to have to decline it. I have my family to consider and my other clients. My time is pretty tight as it is." She watched as his smile disappeared. For some reason she hated being the one who made it vanish.

He coaxed, "I'm sure your husband would understand that it's only for a few weeks. And I don't think it would be so time-consuming you couldn't do your other dictation."

"I don't have a husband." Was there a hint of relief on his face when she said that? "I'm responsible for my brothers."

He leaned forward. "How old are they?"

"In their late teens."

He looked mystified. "Wouldn't they understand you being away some?"

"They probably wouldn't notice but I would." He certainly wasn't going to give up easy.

"What if I pay you double time?" He crossed his arms on his desk.

Her eyes widened. There were hundreds of things she could use that money for. But money wasn't the most important thing in the world. It was nothing like being there for Rick at his games or being around when Mark needed to talk. Particularly with his current frame of mind. His schooling was too important for him to drop out. "I'm sorry. I'm still going to have to say no."

"Is there any way I could convince you?"

"Not now. I'm sorry I can't help you." She looked at her phone. "I really need to go. I'm supposed to be across town in thirty minutes."

"Then you must go," he said in a businesslike tone that still sounded special wrapped in his beautiful baritone.

Cynthia put her purse under her arm and stood.

He leaned back in his chair but didn't come to his feet.

She offered her hand. "I really am sorry."

He stood and took it. His was large and enveloped hers, making her feel tiny yet somehow protected instead of smothered. He said, "I am too. If you change your mind just let me know."

Cynthia nodded. He let her hand go. She felt the loss of warmth immediately. Her knees shook slightly as she walked down the hall. No man should have that kind of effect on her just by touching her hand.

Sean watched Cynthia's ash-brown hair swing across the tops of her shoulders as she walked out of the door. She certainly wasn't the frumpy middle-aged woman he'd anticipated. Instead she was a young vibrant woman who knew her own mind. She was far more interesting than he'd expected. What compelled such a striking woman to become a transcriptionist who stayed behind the scenes? Somehow it didn't fit her. She looked more suited for the front desk.

Cynthia might be short in stature but she was tall in backbone. He like the way her green eyes expressed her feelings. They'd certainly made it clear how she felt about his office. She'd bitten the corner of her mouth as she'd thought about how she was going to answer his questions. He had to give her credit for the diplomatic way she'd done so. Her actions had been endearing, yet telling. He had the feeling she'd found humor in the situation by the small laugh lines that gathered around her eyes.

Sean walked down the hall toward the front of the building, intent on locking the door. The back door opened and shut. His nurse was leaving for the evening but he would be staying for some time to come. As he reached the lobby Cynthia entered.

"Can I change my mind about that job?" There was a note of desperation in her voice.

He was surprised by her question but grateful she was reconsidering. "Sure."

"When would you like me to start?"

He smiled. "Now would be great."

Her face took on an astonished look. "I can't—"

"I don't expect you to start this minute. I'll send you more dictation and some information about what I want. For the most part you should be able to do the work from home but it may require you coming here a few times."

Cynthia nodded. "Okay. That should work."

"May I ask what changed your mind?" She'd seemed firm about her decision earlier.

"I just got a call from my brother and he's having car trouble. This is the second time in two weeks." She shrugged. "Turns out I need the extra money."

"I'm sorry about your car issues." He was but

he was also thankful he'd be getting her assistance. "Can I do anything to help out? Do you need me to call a tow truck?"

She shook her head. "Thank you, but I'm fine for now. Mark has a friend who'll tow the car to our house. Please send over what you need me to do and I'll get started on it right away."

Sean watched her walk toward an older-model car. It was a basic four-door vehicle, practical and efficient. Not unlike his. Cynthia seemed to face her financial responsibilities head-on. That was something he could admire.

The next morning Cynthia checked her email.

Cynthia,

I wanted to make sure you got the car home with no trouble. Please let me know if you need any help. I have a great mechanic and I'd be glad to call him.

I have attached some guidelines for the grant and some files that need to be included. Please let me know if you have any questions.

Again, I appreciate your help.

Sean

She appreciated Sean's offer. The more dealings she had with Dr. Donavon, the better she liked him.

Cynthia noticed he'd signed off as "Sean." She'd told him to call her Cynthia so her guess was he was reciprocating. Did he want her to call him by his first name? He'd not suggested that when they had met. Now all of a sudden he was using his given name. She shouldn't be making such a big deal of it but she liked the idea of them being on a first-name basis.

Cynthia practiced saying his name out loud. It suited him. After all her daydreaming she had to keep in mind that they were merely employee and employer. She didn't need to read more into a simple signature than there was. Still she couldn't ignore the extra clip-clop of her heart when she reread the note.

All these speculations and she still didn't really know anything about the man. He could be married for all she knew. But he hadn't been wearing a ring. But nowadays that didn't mean anything. She hoped he was married. At least she could put an end to her romantic illusions. The reality of a romance between them was laughable. She really needed to get out more. Meet some men. She was spending too much time in a dream world wrapped in a sultry male voice. Reality was what she should concentrate on. Like her brothers attending college and the cost of them staying there or the problem of repairing Mark's car.

Over the next few days she worked hard to get Sean's reports typed and to keep up with her other transcriptions. To her surprise, she enjoyed working on the grant. Found it fascinating. At first it took a great deal of effort to understand what was necessary but she soon became caught up in the brilliant work that Sean was doing. Her being impressed was an understatement.

On Tuesday afternoon, she headed for Sean's office to deliver the work she had finished. Rick's eighteenth birthday was in two days and she was going to take some time off to get ready for it. Pulling into a parking spot, she tried to convince herself she was making the extra effort to turn the reports in just because of the party planning but that wasn't true. She secretly hoped she might see Sean. Especially since she'd taken more care with her hair than usual, not to mention she was now putting on lip gloss.

This is ridiculous.

Cynthia picked up the file and without hesitation got out of the car. She merely had to go in, hand over the papers, return to her vehicle and drive away. She wasn't some teenage girl trying to contrive a way to see a boy. Those days were long gone. Still that tingle of anticipation filled her.

She pulled open the glass door of the lobby, entered and purposely walked to the window. "I'm Cynthia. The transcriptionist. Please see that Dr. Donavon gets these."

The same receptionist who had been there days before took the file. "I will."

Cynthia turned to leave as a middle-aged man entered the lobby from the hallway. Sean was behind him. Her body heated as if she'd gotten caught doing something she shouldn't.

His smile implied he was glad to see her. She returned it.

Sean patted the man on the back. "Good to see you're doing so well, Ralph. I hope to see you again soon." The man headed toward the exit and Sean strolled over to her. "Hi, Cynthia."

"I brought you some reports and the first ten pages of the grant to review." She pointed toward the desk. "I gave them to your receptionist."

"Great. I'll give them a look and let you know if there're any changes to be made. I appreciate you bringing them by."

His voice was even more captivating when she heard it in person. She had to do something more than stand there looking at him. She swallowed. "You're welcome. Well, I'd better go."

"I'll be in touch," Sean said.

And I'll be looking forward to it. Somehow she managed to keep herself from saying it out loud.

The two days she'd taken off turned into busy ones. She'd made arrangements for Rick's birthday and finished some chores she'd been putting off. Everything was set for the party now. All she had to do was load the car and head to the paintball field. She was expecting about twenty teenagers, both boys and girls. Normally she, Mark and Rick celebrated with cake and ice cream with a few friends but this was a special birthday. Now that she had some extra money from overtime she had decided to splurge a little.

With a couple of hours before they needed to leave, Cynthia decided to check her email and review what she would need to get done the next day. She opened her account.

With a giddy feeling she shouldn't be experiencing, she saw one from Sean. She opened it.

Hi Cynthia,

I hope you're having a good day. I've had something come up and I need to get Charles Chadworth's surgical report. It's particular to the grant and I need a colleague to review it. He's leaving on a two-week vacation tomorrow but has said he can look at it tonight. Do you have it completed?

I know this is above and beyond the call of duty, but could you have it ready for a messenger at four p.m.? I must get it to him right away.

Thank you.

Sean

She checked the time. There was just enough for her to type it but no one would be here to give it to the messenger.

She replied.

I can get it typed, but today is my brother's birthday and I'm giving him a party. I won't be here for the messenger when he comes.

Since it's personal information I'm not comfortable leaving it on the porch unattended… I could bring it by your office around nine tonight. Would that do?
Cynthia

Half an hour later she had the report finished and another email from Sean popped into her box.

That's not going to work. I really need it sooner.

Let me see if I can find someone in the office who can come get it.
I'll get back to you.
Sean

She couldn't miss Rick's party or be late. She was the hostess. Had the responsibility of being the designated adult in charge. At one time that title made her feel important. Now it was more of a weight on her shoulders.

Cynthia checked the time. She needed to get going but she also needed to wait to hear from Sean. Ten minutes went by before he replied.

No messenger can make it and there's no one in the office who can do it either.
Can I meet you somewhere and pick it up?
Sean

Cynthia slipped the two sheets of paper into a protective envelope. The report really must be important if he was willing to go to the trouble of personally picking it up.

You'll need to come to 5182 Falcon Road, Bessemer, Al.

Sean replied right away.

I'll see you there.
Thanks for doing this on such short notice.
Sean

Cynthia couldn't help the excitement bubbling in her. She was going to see Sean again. It had been a long time since she'd acted like a woman excited about seeing a man.

* * *

Sean couldn't believe it when he pulled up to the address that Cynthia had given him. It was a large field full of building façades, lean-tos and barrels spaced out at intervals. In a grassy area beside a building no larger than a backyard garden shed, vehicles were parked in a line. Most were jacked-up trucks with the occasional car mixed in.

What was going on here?

He parked next to a red truck. Among the buildings and other obstacles were people dressed in white painter coveralls and wearing clear masks over their faces. They were running from place to place while being shot at with guns that used exploding paintballs.

Why was Cynthia here?

He slowly approached the shed where a couple of teenagers stood laughing and pointing at what was happening on the field. Posted on the siding of the building was a sign stating "Peek's Paintball". Below the sign was a list of the charges for a game, with or without the rental of the equipment. This was just the type of entertainment he didn't waste his money on.

There was nothing to show for the expense. Yet, it seemed several kids and, apparently, Cynthia were playing.

Sean joined the boys. “Hey.”

They looked at him curiously. Was it that obvious he was out of his element? “Do either one of you know where I can find Cynthia Marcum?”

One boy looked at the other. “Isn’t that Rick’s sister?”

“Yeah.” The teen pointed toward the field. “She’s out there somewhere.”

Sean studied the game area, trying to catch a glimpse of Cynthia. Players continued moving between obstacles while being shot at.

“They just started a new game a few minutes ago. It may be a while before she shows up,” one of the boys stated.

Sean didn’t really have time to stand around waiting on her. Cynthia knew he was coming. Why wasn’t she available? “Could you point me in the direction of where you last saw her?”

The taller of the two indicated the right side of the field.

Sean started in that direction.

"Hey, man," the shorter boy called, "I wouldn't do that without a mask and gun. It's an unwritten rule that anyone on the field is fair game."

Sean hesitated. Surely no one would shoot an unarmed man. He wasn't even dressed the part.

"I'll let you have mine. You really don't want to go out there without some protection." The second boy handed him his plastic helmet.

Sean took it. "Thanks. You really think they'd shoot me?"

Both boys gave him a solemn nod.

The tall one asked, "Do you know how to use a paintball gun?"

Sean looked at the clear gun with a black plastic container attached to the bottom and a small black canister on the back. "No, not really."

"This one is an automatic. All you have to do is pull the trigger. This is the hopper." He pointed to the plastic container. "It holds the paintballs. This is your gas." He put his hand on the canister. "You should have plenty. Just point and shoot. Aim for the body."

They had to be kidding. Surely Cynthia wasn't

out there dressed as they were and armed. "Is all of this really necessary?"

Both boys bobbed their heads in a rapid motion.

"Oh, and don't take your mask off for any reason until the whistle blows. Paintballs can leave nasty whelps."

"Got it." Sean started out into the field again. He hadn't gone six feet before he felt a thump and dampness on his upper arm. He looked down to see a bright yellow splatter on his good navy pullover. At least he was wearing jeans. Moving into a trot, he found cover behind a barrel. There were two pinging sounds against the side as he crouched down. Paint flew in the air around him.

A couple of giggles came from a nearby lean-to. He peeked out to see two girls.

"Almost got you," one called.

"Do you know where Cynthia Marcum is?" Sean brought his head back, not moving from his sheltered spot.

"Whose team are you on?" came a response.

"No one's. I came here to see Cynthia." He'd had no idea it would be this hard to do.

"She's guarding our fort," a girl called.

"Fort?" He hadn't seen anything that looked like a fort among the structures.

"Yeah. It's the church," another voice called. "You better be careful. She's a good shot."

"We're going to believe you this time. We'll let you by," one of the girls called.

"Thanks. I appreciate that." Sean stood but kept his head low as he ran toward the façade that looked like a white church front with a steeple. When he was hit in the hip, he took cover behind some boards driven into the ground forming a haphazard fence. Okay, he'd had all the paint on him he wanted. It was time to retaliate.

Sean did a three-sixty survey of the area. A boy came into his field of vision and Sean pulled the trigger. With a pop, pop, pop the balls left the chamber. Two hit the ground near the boy's feet. He turned to run and the third caught him square in the back.

A smile covered Sean's lips. This game might be more interesting than he'd thought. He ran across an open area to another barrel, fully expecting to draw fire. When none came his confidence increased and he kept moving. He reached a large oak tree that stood in the middle of the field and stopped, waited.

Where was Cynthia? He needed to get that report and get back to his office. There was still work to do tonight. Sean yelled, "Cynthia?"

Seconds later he heard, "Over here."

She was at the church. Sean headed in that direction. This time he wasn't as lucky as he had been during his last run. A couple of boys stepped out from behind a storefront and paintballs sailed in his direction. Ducking and zigzagging, he ran behind the church front and straight into someone.

With a grunt from him and a whoosh from the person he hit, they landed with a thud on the ground in a tangle of legs and arms. Seconds later he looked into the wide, dazed eyes of Cynthia. Their mouths were close enough to touch if not for the plastic masks between them. Sean wished he could kiss her. Almost instantly behind that thought came the realization of how soft the feminine curves were beneath him. When she shifted, they became even more evident.

"Uh…Sean, what're you doing here?" Cynthia looked at him as if she might be imagining him.

"Do you mean here on top of you or here as in on the playing field?"

For a moment she looked perplexed, as if she didn't understand the question. "Both, I think."

"I was looking for you. You told me to meet you here." She really did have beautiful eyes.

Cynthia struggled to get out from under him. "I don't think I asked you to knock me down and lay on me."

"No. That was purely accidental." *And my pleasure.* He rolled to his side, taking some of the pressure off her. She shimmied against him. His body warmed and twitched in awareness. A movement above them caught his attention. He glanced up. A boy pointing a gun was bearing down on them.

Suddenly Cynthia twisted to her side and away from him. "I have to protect the fort," she muttered with a sound of determination as she reached for her gun.

Sean raised his and aimed. The paintball hit the boy in the chest. Red paint covered his coverall.

"Aw, Cyn, I was so close," the kid said with disappointment in his voice.

Cynthia giggled. "Yet so far away." She looked back at him. "Thanks, Doc, nice shot."

"You're welcome." Sean grinned as he got to his feet. He offered her a hand. She took it without hesitation. "There's a first time for everything." He'd impressed not only himself but her as well. He liked that for some reason. He was confident she didn't suffer fools easily.

"Really? You've never played paintball?" She looked around them as if making sure no one else was headed in their direction.

"No." This was just the type of thing that there was never money for when he was growing up. He would have loved to have had a birthday party like this one, or even gone to one, but more times than not there was barely money for food. His parents had told him more than once it would get better after the "new business" took off. That had never happened.

The boy walked back the way Sean had come.

"So is he done?" Sean asked.

"Yeah, he got hit in the chest so he has to sit out now." Cynthia crouched behind the church supports. “I’d have you on my team any time.” Admiration filled her voice.

He involuntarily puffed out his chest and stood straighter.

Her attention had already returned to the field. She glanced back at him and pulled at his arm. “Hey, you better get down or you’re going to have more paint on you than you already have.” A second passed. “Why don’t you have on coveralls? You have ruined your sweater and jeans.”

“I hadn’t planned on wallowing on the ground or being shot at by kids. Some guy told me not to come out here without a mask and gun. He didn’t offer me coveralls. I’m here for a report, not to be a target. By the way, when’re you going to be free here so I can get my report?”

“It shouldn’t take long.” She looked around the façade as if she expected someone was sneaking up on them. “My team should be returning any minute now.”

He looked. “Just how do you tell who’s on your team?”

“By the color on their helmet.” She made it sound as if anyone should know that. His chest deflated.

No other women he knew would be out here playing this game. "You have to be kidding. That means they must get pretty close before you know if they are friend or foe?"

"Yep. But that's part of the fun." Cynthia sounded as if she loved the challenge.

He guessed it was. To his surprise he was having a good time.

"So why exactly are you here?"

"They were short one team member and I got drafted. I'm just filling in on this game until one of Rick's friends shows up."

That made sense. But Sean had already gotten too caught up in this craziness.

Her focus remained on the field around them. "I'll be done here in a few minutes."

She sure took the game seriously. It sounded as if no amount of prodding on his part was going to change her mind. She looked cute in the baggy white paper coveralls with her hair pulled back by the mask and her eyes wide in anticipation. His type was usually the "I can't get my fingernails broken or my shoes dirty" kind, and here he was admiring a woman with no makeup and paint all over her.

A tall, lanky boy ran toward them calling with excitement, "Hey, Cyn. We won. I got the last of them."

Cynthia stood. "Great."

Sean joined her.

"This has been the best birthday party ever. Thanks." The boy stopped in front of them and gave Cynthia a hug.

She returned it. "I'm glad you like it." Cynthia pulled off her mask and shook out her hair.

Sean could do little more than stare. She looked so sexy as her hair floated around her shoulders. His body heated. By the way she acted, Cynthia had no idea how captivating the action was. He was more aware with each passing second. Why was he reacting to her so? This wasn't like him.

There had been women in his life. Plenty of them but none had interested him enough to cause this type of response in such a short time. His female companions had been just that. Companions. Some for the night, others for a month or two. He wanted a woman who was serious, focused. Thought like he did. After living with his parents he'd learned too well that some people haphazardly went through life. He planned, considered each step.

Sean knew the value of hard work and used his money wisely. Unlike this party. No matter how entertaining it might be, he couldn't see why Cynthia would spend so much on a party when he was sure she could have used the money elsewhere. Like repairing her brother's car. He could already tell she wasn't the person for him but still he liked her. What would it hurt to enjoy her company while it lasted?

"Sean, I'd like you to meet my youngest brother, Rick. It's his birthday we're celebrating. Rick, this is Dr. Donavon." She put a hand on her brother's arm.

The affection between them was obvious. Something that Sean and his siblings didn't share. He hadn't seen his older brother and sister in a couple of years. He'd been much younger and so different from them that their relationships hadn't been close. Sean had been an outsider in his own family. The idea that his brother or sister would throw him a party was laughable.

"Nice to meet you, Rick. Happy birthday."

Sean offered his hand. The boy had a firm handshake. "Please call me Sean."

Cynthia gave him a warm smile. She seemed to appreciate him allowing her brother the familiarity. There were too many confusing emotions surrounding him liking that idea that he chose not to contemplate it further.

Cynthia handed her headgear and gun to Rick. "Will you see about these? I've got to get a report out of the car for Sean."

"Uh, sure." Rick took the equipment. Rick turned to him. "I can take yours too."

Flipping the mask off, Sean handed it and the gun to Rick. "It belongs to some guy with red hair who was standing up by the shed."

"That'd be Johnny. I'll see that he gets it." Rick headed in the direction he'd come.

"Let's go. My car is over here," Cynthia said as she walked toward what he assumed was the car park.

Sean followed. Even in the coveralls, Cynthia had a nice swing to her hips. She had a generous behind that proclaimed she was all woman.

This interest in her had to stop.

CHAPTER THREE

CYNTHIA GLANCED AROUND at Sean. A look of guilt flickered in his eyes. Had she just caught him checking her out?

Her spine tingled. There had been a moment just like it when he'd been on top of her. He was affecting her in ways she wasn't completely comfortable with. What was going on? This couldn't continue. He was in truth her boss and even if he wasn't they lived in two different worlds.

She made her strides longer. He should be sent on his way as soon as possible. There wasn't time in her life to think about Sean Donavon. Her brothers and keeping their financial heads above water were all she needed to focus on. Her life didn't need muddling by dreamy thoughts of Sean.

Thankfully they soon reached her car. But then she realized she had to remove her coveralls to get her keys out of her jeans. Distressed, she tried to make it clean and simple, instead of the striptease she was afraid it might look like. Cynthia didn't miss the slight uplift to Sean's lips when she wiggled back and forth as she struggled to remove the material from her shoulders. He was appreciating the spectacle she was making.

"A gentleman would offer to help," she snapped as she continued to twist.

He grinned. "I was sort of enjoying the show."

Heat rose to her cheeks.

Sean stepped closer, which didn't help matters in the least. He gave her collar a tug.

"Thanks."

"My pleasure." He sounded sincere.

The panic that had simmered while she worked to undress had started to flame. Cynthia let the coveralls drop to her feet and dug into her pocket for her keys. Finding them, she laid them on the top of the car then pulled the coveralls up and tied the sleeves around her waist.

"So did you get the car you were having trouble with fixed?" Sean asked.

"It's running but my pocketbook is empty." She clicked the car door opener.

"I bet having this party at the same time didn't help." His tone was matter-of-fact.

Was he being critical? Did he think she was wasting money? "You're not kidding. But Rick only turns eighteen once. He deserved a nice party. Some fun."

"Maybe."

Sean didn't sound as if he agreed. "Anyway, it's good for you. It just means that you'll have me for as long as you need me." Grabbing the file off the seat, she almost shoved it at him.

Something about the slight twist of his lips confused her. It was as if she was talking about one thing while he was thinking of another. A tremor washed through her body at the thought of him touching her. She hoped her reaction didn't show. The man had her tied up in knots in more ways than one.

"Thanks." He took the file in his hand.

"Cyn, come quick!" Rick, still dressed in playing gear, ran toward them waving his arm. "Ann Marie is hurt."

"What's wrong?" Cynthia called.

The boy yelled, "She's hurt her leg."

"Tell her not to move. I'll be right there." Cynthia dug under the car seat, pulling out a first-aid kit. When she stood she didn't see Sean anywhere. Seconds later she was trotting toward Rick. At the sound of footsteps, she glanced to her right to find Sean beside her.

At what must have been her questioning look he said, "I thought I might help."

"Thanks." She was grateful. If Ann Marie was badly injured she could really use his medical assistance.

They rounded a stack of drums on the playing field to find Rick on bended knee beside a girl. She was still wearing coveralls but her mask lay beside her. Her blond hair fell loosely down her back as she rubbed the ankle of her left leg. A couple of other kids stood looking down as her with interest.

Cynthia joined them and went down on her knees. "Ann Marie, I'm Cynthia. Rick's sister. What hurts?"

"My ankle. I can't walk." The girl's pain was obvious.

Focusing on nothing else but Ann Marie, Cynthia put a hand on her shoulder, hoping to reassure her. "Let me look. Where exactly does it hurt?"

"Right here," the girl cried out as she touched the spot.

Moving down to where she could easily reach Ann Marie's foot, Cynthia began to push the pants leg of the coveralls up. "You let me know if I'm hurting you." She slowly gathered the material until she could see the ankle area. "I'm going to need to roll your sock down."

The girl shifted.

"Stay still. You wouldn't want to make the injury worse." Cynthia carefully touched Ann Marie's skin, checking around the ankle bone for raised areas or tenderness. When her fingers reached the skin on the inside of Ann Marie's ankle she winced.

Cynthia shifted, getting a better view. Even in the dimming afternoon light she could make out a purple discoloration of the skin. Her fingers moved to the strings of Ann Marie's shoe.

"Don't do that," Sean's stern voice told her. He joined her on the ground.

Cynthia had forgotten all about him. She was surprised he hadn't said something sooner or taken over the situation. She gave him a questioning look.

"It could be broken. The shoe will act as a splint," he explained. "It should remain on and be removed at the emergency department."

That made sense. Cynthia sat back on her heels and spoke to Ann Marie. "You have definitely sprained it or worse. We're going to have to make a trip to the ER."

The teen started crying.

Cynthia lightly patted her leg, trying to comfort her. "You're going to be fine."

The girl gave her a tear-filled look. "My parents are going to be so mad at me. They told me not to come to the party."

A knot formed in Cynthia's stomach. She wasn't looking forward to the conversation to come. "I'm sure they'll understand. Right now let's worry about that ankle. We need to get you to the car and on to the hospital."

"I want to stabilize the foot more before she's moved just on the off chance it's broken," Sean said.

Cynthia turned to him. "How do we do that?"

"We need something to wrap around the shoe

that will support the ankle. A long piece of cloth, anything." Sean looked at her then above them at the others watching.

"I have an old knit scarf in my car—would that do?" a girl offered softly.

"That'd be great." Sean gave her a reassuring smile.

"I'll run get it." The girl didn't wait for a response before she took off at a full run toward the parking lot.

"I'm going to need to roll up your pants leg so that we can keep it out of the way. I need to wrap your foot securely. This shouldn't hurt." Sean's large hands went to work on neatly folding the material. "So what grade are you in?"

"Eleventh."

He nodded. "What's your favorite subject?"

"I like English," Ann Marie responded.

Sean continued to work. "That so?"

Cynthia watched. Sean had a nice bedside manner about him. One that she could easily fall for as well. Ann Marie had stopped crying and was now concentrating on answering Sean's questions.

Minutes later the girl returned with a scarf

balled up in her hand. Reaching them, she thrust it at Sean. Taking it, he smoothed out the width and length, then placed one end under Ann Marie's foot and started covering it as if he were using an elastic bandage. He then brought it up around her ankle and secured it under a section he'd already wrapped.

Sean pushed to his feet. "Now off to Emergency you go. Rick, will you get behind Ann Marie and help lift her up while I pull her from here? Ann Marie, don't for any reason put weight on that foot."

Rick moved into position.

Sean said, "Ready, set, go."

Cynthia helped steady Ann Marie as Sean and Rick got her up on one foot. Before she had a chance to wobble, Sean had scooped her into his arms and had her held against his chest.

Speaking to Rick, she said, "I'm going to take Ann Marie to the hospital and stay with her until her parents get there."

"We'll go in my car. I saw all the birthday stuff in the backseat of yours," Sean said.

He didn't sound as if he would allow any argument. She nodded and told Rick, "You drive my car home. I'll be there as soon as I see about Ann Marie. You can have cake and ice cream here. It's in the car. The ice cream's in the cooler in the trunk."

"I'll take care of it," one of the girls called as Cynthia hurried to catch up with Sean, who was already headed toward the parking area. "Ann Marie, I'll save you some for when you get home."

Ann Marie gave the girl a weak wave.

"Thanks," Cynthia said, over her shoulder. Nearing a midsized four-door car that Sean was obviously headed for, she hurried past him to open the back door. It was locked.

"The keys are in my pocket. You're going to have to get them."

What? She wasn't going to stick her hand in his pants pocket.

"I can hold An—"

Sean gave her a stern look. "They're in my right pocket. Get them."

Cynthia stepped around him. Swallowing hard, she slowly slipped her hand into the top of his front pocket. Thankfully Sean's pants weren't super tight. His body tensed. The hiss of air told her Sean wasn't unaffected by her actions.

She bit down on her lower lip as her hand continued to push farther along his leg. Her fingers found the keys and jerked them out. Cynthia released the breath she had been holding, unlocked the doors, and opened the rear one.

Sean worked to sit Ann Marie on the seat in the small confined space. Cynthia went around to the other side and, by putting her hands under the girl's arms, pulled her across the seat. "Ann Marie, I'm going to close the door and you can lean against it. It won't be a comfortable ride but your leg and foot need to rest straight on the seat."

She watched as Sean quickly pulled his sweater off. A hint of a firm abdomen showed above his beltline when his shirt came untucked. She hated to admit her disappointment when it disappeared as his arms came down from over his head.

"Here." He wadded the sweater up and handed it to Ann Marie. "You can use this to cushion your back against the door handle." Cynthia closed the door and watched through the window to make sure the girl was settled before she started around the car to the front passenger seat. The other car door slammed, and Sean met her halfway around the car.

"Thanks for your help," Cynthia said.

"Not a problem." Sean continued to the driver's side.

Half an hour later, Sean drove up to the entrance of Emergency Department and stopped. He hopped out of the car and circled it to find Cynthia at the rear door with it already open. She was helping Ann Marie to slide across the seat.

"Don't let her stand. I'm going to get an orderly and a wheelchair." Sean headed toward the sliding glass doors.

"We'll be right here," Cynthia called after him.

Minutes later he returned pulling a rolling bed while a member of the medical staff pushed it. They positioned it beside the car. With the wheel brakes on, Sean said, "Cynthia, if you would help scoot Ann Marie as far to the edge of the seat as you can, then I'll lift her onto the rolling bed."

Sean waited until Cynthia had the girl in position. Supporting her back with one arm and the other under her knees, he lifted Ann Marie gently and placed her on the bed. Turning to Cynthia, he handed her his keys. "Why don't you park my car? I'll see to Ann Marie. I have a buddy who's an ortho guy. I'm going to give him a call."

"Okay. I'll be there in a minute."

Sean didn't have to wait long before Cynthia joined him in the examination room. She'd removed her coveralls and now wore a sweatshirt with a local college insignia on the front and jeans. She looked about the same age as Ann Marie.

The orderly finished settling the girl. "The doctor's on her way in."

Sean said, "I've already phoned Dr. Mills. He has agreed to consult. He should be here soon."

Cynthia immediately stepped to the bedside. "Are you feeling any pain?"

"It throbs," Ann Marie said quietly.

Cynthia patted her hand. "I'm sure they'll do X-rays and have you out of here in no time."

"I hope so. Mama and Dad are not going to be happy when they see me." The girl seemed more concerned about her parents than she was about her foot.

While on their way he and Cynthia had listened as Ann Marie called and told her parents what had happened and which hospital she was being taken to. Her mother's voice could be heard loud and clear from the backseat. She wasn't happy.

"I'm sure they'll just be glad you weren't hurt worse," Cynthia assured her.

Soon a tech from X-ray entered and whisked Ann Marie away leaving him and Cynthia in the empty room.

"Uh, here're your keys." She pulled them from her pocket and handed them to him. Her cheeks went pink. Was she thinking of when she'd had to fish them out of his pocket?

Sean took them. Her hand touched his for a split second. Even that sent an electric shock through him. What was it with this woman? "You did a nice job out there with Ann Marie. It looked like you've had first-aid training."

She moved to "her" side of the room, as if they were boxers facing off but unsure of the next move. "More like nursing training."

"Really? You're in nursing school?"

"I was, or was planning to be. I took nursing classes in high school. I was going to college to be a RN." Cynthia took one of the two chairs in the small space. She sat straight in her chair with her hands in her lap as if she wasn't completely comfortable around him.

"Well, it showed. You were cool, calm and collected." Sean meant it. He'd been impressed. If he hadn't stepped in, he was sure she'd still have been able to handle the situation.

Cynthia looked at him. "You did a nice job on wrapping her foot. Quick thinking."

He shrugged and grinned. "I have had some medical training after all."

"Wrap a lot of noses in scarves, do ya?"

He laughed. "Not so many. There's always a first time for everything."

"You get an A plus for effort. I do appreciate you driving us over and having your friend see Ann Marie. I know you had other plans tonight. Please don't feel like you have to stay."

Sean leaned back against the wall and crossed his arms over his chest. "Trying to get rid of me?"

"No, but I know you're concerned about that

grant application. And time is tight. You must need to go."

He checked his watch. He did have to meet Charles soon but he still had time. "I'm good. I have the report with me. I'll call my colleague and make new arrangements. I want to make sure Ann Marie doesn't need me to cut any red tape before I leave."

"You have the report with you?"

"Yeah. I stuck it in my car while you were hunting for the first-aid kit."

There was a commotion in the hall. The door to the room opened and a middle-aged couple hurried in. It could only be Ann Marie's parents. Sean straightened and Cynthia stood.

She took a step toward the couple. Sean came to stand behind her as she said, "Mr. and Mrs. Lucas, I'm Cynthia Marcum. Rick's sister. I want to assure you that Ann Marie is doing fine. She's having an X-ray done now."

The woman took a threatening step toward Cynthia. "How could you've let this happen? I told Ann Marie she couldn't come to the party. There wouldn't be enough supervision with just you there. I blame you for this."

Cynthia recoiled until her back met his chest. Sean felt a slight tremor roll through her. His neck stiffened. What was he missing here? He wasn't going to allow anyone to talk to her that way.

"I can assure you that Ms. Marcum has taken and still is taking extremely good care of Ann Marie. What happened to Ann Marie was merely an accident." Stepping around Cynthia, he put himself between the irate mother and her. "I'm Dr. Sean Donavon. She handled the situation admirably. Ann Marie is doing fine."

Cynthia shifted to stand ridged beside him. She was going to stand her own ground, it appeared. "Mr. and Mrs. Lucas, I can assure you that your daughter has been under *continuous* supervision and has had *capable* care. She took a fall and twisted her ankle. We brought her here only as a precaution. I'm sorry it happened but she's doing fine. She'll be back here in a few minutes."

"I told Dan—" the mother glanced at her husband before turning her leer on Cynthia again "—that Ann Marie wasn't to go to the party. I just knew something like this would happen," she hissed.

Sean's shoulders relaxed when he saw Ann Marie being pushed into the room, ending the conversation. He touched Cynthia's shoulder and nodded toward the far wall. She joined him out of the way. Cynthia must be as glad the discussion was over as he was. His jaw was tight in an effort not to say what he really thought to the over-the-top mother. Ann Marie's father hadn't said anything. Sean wasn't surprised; he couldn't be anything but browbeaten.

The mother hurried to the bedside, hardly letting the transporter get the bed back into position. "Oh, honey, are you okay? I told you that you had no business at that party."

"Rick is my friend," Ann Marie whined.

"Yes, but you know how we feel about his family," the mother said in a tight voice, glaring at Cynthia.

"Mama, hush," Ann Marie hissed.

Sean had heard enough. He hated to leave the young girl to fend for herself but his and Cynthia's presence wasn't helping the situation. "Ann Marie, Cynthia and I will go now that your parents are here. We'll call and check on you. Let me know if you have any problems. My buddy Dr. David Mills will be in here soon to look at your foot. He's a nice guy. You'll like him. Get him to show you a picture of his pet ferret."

Ann Marie gave him a weak smile. "Thanks, Sean. Cynthia. Sorry I messed up the party."

Cynthia stepped to the bed with shoulders squared and head high as if she were daring the girl's parents to say anything. "You don't worry about that. We'll have plenty of ice cream and cake left. When you get home I'll send Rick over with some."

"That sounds great."

Cynthia went out of the door ahead of him. They stopped at the nurses' station, where he let them know he was leaving and that Ann Marie's parents had arrived.

"What was that all about?" he asked as soon as they were out of earshot of everyone.

"I guess it's about the fact that I am responsible for my two brothers and that Ann Marie's parents don't think I'm doing a good enough job. I appreciate your support back there. You're a good guy, Dr. Sean Donavon."

Was this feeling of pride in his chest the same one as a knight of old experienced when he saved a damsel in distress? He sure hoped so; he rather liked it. "I know it's been an emotional few hours and you're probably ready to get home but I need to run this report upstairs to my buddy's office."

Cynthia gave him a weary look. "It's not a problem. I'll just wait in the car."

"You sure? You could ride up with me if you want." Sean hated to leave her sitting in the car.

She took a second to answer. "Okay."

"I'll go out and get it."

"I'll go with you," Cynthia said in a sad voice. He wished he could put that upbeat sound back into it. "I need to walk off this anger I'm feeling ever since Mrs. Lucas showed up. My parents would be so upset to know someone thought so poorly of our family."

Hoping to make her feel better, Sean said, "I, for one, would consider the source or give her the benefit of the doubt because her child was hurt and forget it."

"I wish it was that easy."

His gaze didn't leave her face. "I know it isn't."

They walked to the car, he got his file and they returned to the building. He led her to a staff elevator and they rode to the fifth floor. There they walked down the hall to where there were a group of nondescript doors.

Sean knocked on one of them. A voice called, “Come in.”

Sean glanced back at her and she said, “I’ll just wait out here.”

A few minutes later he joined her again. “All done. Let’s go.”

She nodded and they headed back down the hall toward the elevator. On it once again, Sean looked her as she took a spot on the opposite side of the car. Studying her as she watched the floor numbers light up, he noticed a small blob of yellow in her hair. “You have some paint just at your temple.”

Cynthia pushed at her hair but missed the spot.

He reached out and brushed his fingers against her skin. Sean didn’t miss the catch in her breathing as his hand continued into her hair. Removing the paint, he showed it to her on the end of his fingers. “See?”

She looked at him wide-eyed as if all her

senses were on alert. His certainly were. Cynthia smelled of grass, sunshine and a hint of something that could only be hers alone. Her skin had been smooth as a flower petal. She looked wild and vulnerable in her sweatshirt and jeans with her hair slightly disheveled.

A whispered “Oh” escaped her lips.

The only sense he hadn’t experienced was her taste. He wanted to. Would it be as good as he’d imagined? He leaned forward, his mouth moving toward hers. The bell of the elevator announced they had reached the lobby.

Cynthia jerked back, and he straightened. He’d been so close to what he was searching for. A charmingly guilty look came over her face as three people stood on the outside of the elevator looking at them. She hurried out. He followed more slowly.

Sean was feeling anything but embarrassment. It was more like need, want, desire, lust…

Cynthia was still trembling from the almost kiss when they reached Sean’s car. Even in her fantasies she’d not gone that far. Had he really been going to kiss her? She would never have thought a man like Sean would ever be interested in her. With his looks and beautiful voice a tall, leggy blonde who wore tight dresses seemed more his style. Yet, he'd almost kissed her and she hoped he tried again. Soon.

Sean was ready to pull out of the parking lot when she said, "I live out in Bessemer."

He nodded and turned into the traffic headed south. "I didn't want to ask until we were alone but would you mind telling me about what happened to your parents?"

She didn't want to go into her family dynamics but Sean deserved an explanation. She looked out of the window, but not really seeing anything. "My parents died a few years ago in a car accident. Since I was of age I assumed guardianship of my brothers. It hasn't been easy all the time. Mark hasn't always stayed within the lines but we're still together."

"Mark?"

"Yeah. My other brother. He is in college and has a part-time job. He had to work this evening. He should be at home when we get there."

Sean glanced at her. "How old is he?"

"About to turn twenty," she said in a flat tone.

"No wonder. He was about, what, seventeen when your parents died? Hard age to lose your parents."

"Day after his eighteenth birthday. He took it hard. We all did." She hadn't talked about this in a long time. She had focused on living. Making each day the best she could for herself and her brothers. Now they were both adults but she still felt a responsibility to see they had a good start in life. Saw fun in life.

"So how old were you when you became their guardian?"

"Twenty-one."

He let out a long whistle. "That had to be tough."

"Not really. I was determined our family would stay together. I wouldn't have had it any other way." It hadn't been. She knew what she had to do and had done it.

"I'm impressed. Not everyone's willing to sacrifice like that."

She couldn't imagine anyone not putting their family first. "I was taught that family was everything. I was not going to let us be split up. The boys needed to stay in the same school, have the same friends, stay in the only home they have known."

"So you gave up nursing school to take care of them?"

She shrugged. "Not gave it up as much as postponed it. I did what had to be done at the time. Nursing school could wait." She would do the same again.

"It seems that a lot would have to wait to devote your life to others for years." He said it as if he'd never known someone who'd sacrificed for their family. Or couldn't believe that anyone would.

Thankfully traffic was light and they were turning into her drive only a few minutes later. Her family home was a simple one-story brick on a tree-lined street in a rural neighborhood. Nothing special but it was theirs. She liked this time of day when lights shone through the windows of the other houses. It gave her a sense of security to know she was surrounded by others.

When he'd turned off the engine she turned to him. "I can't say thanks enough for your help."

He smiled. "I have to admit it was a different

evening for me. Especially the paintball. It was fun." Sean sounded surprised by that.

"Even the part where you had to take Ann Marie to the hospital?" Sean really was a gorgeous man. But she'd found other things to like about him besides his looks and voice. He'd been great with Ann Marie, even more amazing with her parents.

Sean shrugged and chuckled. "Every doctor loves a trip to the hospital."

She laughed. "I guess they do. I'm glad you were there. Having a doctor along in an emergency is reassuring." Add another positive. A good sport. She could fall for this guy. And that idea was crazy.

"It wasn't like you needed me. You could have handled it." He glanced at the house.

"I appreciate the vote of confidence. Would you like to come in for some cake and ice cream? It's not much in the way of a thank-you but it's the best I can do."

CHAPTER FOUR

SEAN HADN'T BEEN planning to get out of the car. He'd had every intention of dropping Cynthia off and heading for his office as soon as possible. But for some reason he didn't want to leave her company yet. Wanted to know more about her.

He checked his watch. There was time. Staying here and having dessert with Cynthia was much more appealing than wading through paperwork but it wasn't like him to take time away from a project. He shook his head. He couldn't believe he was even considering it. Grinning, he said, "Sure. I'm always up for cake and ice cream."

Before he could get out and close the door Cynthia was on her way up the walk. "I want to make sure you can get into the house. The boys aren't always good about tidying up."

A short time later he joined her in the living room. There was nothing special about the area.

The chairs, sofa and TV were what he expected, yet there was an air of being lived in that he'd not experienced in a room since he'd left home. A family lived here. Why had he thought of his own family now?

"Come back this way to the kitchen." Cynthia headed down a small hallway into a yellow room with the lights already on. On the wooden table sitting in a bay window was a cake box and a couple of plastic grocery bags.

"Hey, Cyn, that you?" a voice called from somewhere in the house.

"Yeah," she said over her shoulder.

Seconds later Rick came to stand in the doorway. Nodding to him, Rick said to Cynthia, "How's Ann Marie?"

"She should be fine. Her parents showed up and we left." Cynthia looked into the cake box.

"They're a piece of work, aren't they?" Rick stepped further into the room.

"They're just concerned about their daughter." Cynthia opened the bags and searched inside.

Sean twisted up his mouth. She was being generous toward them in his opinion. He'd seen people upset in his profession but those two had lashed out undeservingly at Cynthia.

She turned to Rick. “I’m sorry I had to miss part of the party.”

“I understand. It was still a great one. Best I’ve had since Mom and Dad died.”

Cynthia gave him a smile that Sean couldn’t quite put a name to. One that contained both happiness and grief. Maybe the money she’d spent hadn’t been so wasteful. It had certainly made her brother happy.

That was an odd thought for him. He’d spent most of his adult life being thrifty and practical about money. Before today you could have never persuaded him that playing paintball was a good use of hard-earned money.

“I’m glad. I wanted it to be a good one. I think we owe Sean some cake and ice cream for helping us out.” Cynthia looked back at the cake.

Rick nodded. “Yeah, sure. Thanks, Sean.”

“You’re welcome, Rick. Again, happy birthday.”

“You want to join us?” Cynthia asked her brother.

“Naw,” he said. “I’ll wait to have some with

Mark when he gets home. He called to say he had to work overtime. He said I'm really going to like his birthday gift. I'm going to call and see if Ann Marie is home yet." The boy disappeared down the hall.

Sean chuckled. "I think he might be interested in more than her ankle."

Cynthia grinned. "I believe you might be right."

She had a nice smile. One that when directed at him he liked too much. Thoughts of their almost-kiss surfaced. Would her mouth be as warm and inviting as it looked?

"How about that ice cream and cake?" Cynthia pulled a paper plate with balloons on it out of one of the bags.

"Sure. But I can't stay long. I still have work to do."

"My guess is that you don't take time off much." Cynthia served him a large piece of cake.

"I have a busy medical practice. It requires my attention." He took the plate she handed him and sat on a chair at the table.

She cut a much smaller piece and placed it in front of the empty chair next to him. "I know that but having down time, fun, is important too."

"I have fun." Sean watched as she went to the freezer and pulled out a round tub of ice cream.

"Doing what? You've never played paintball until today." She opened a cabinet drawer, took out a large spoon and two smaller ones, then closed it.

"A lot of people have never played paintball." Sean failed to understand how that equated to not ever having fun. He'd not played those types of things as a kid because there hadn't been money to do them with. When he'd got older he'd had to go to work. Then there had been medical school. Games weren't something he'd had time for or extra money to waste on.

"That's true. So, what do you like to do for fun?"

Sean was ashamed to admit he had to really think long and too hard for an answer. He didn't have a hobby. His job was his life. It was what would provide him security. Fun wasn't even on his list of needs. "I like to fix noses."

She scoffed. "That's your job. What do you do outside of being a doctor?"

"I like to read."

"Okay, that can be fun. Anything else?" Cynthia looked at him expectantly. As if his having fun was of super importance to her.

"I own a bike." Which he hadn't ridden in weeks.

Her face lit up. "I'm impressed. Riding around here with the mountains and all must be a real workout."

He took another bite of cake. The few times he'd taken the time to ride he had found it invigorating. "It can be. I like to bike in Mountain Brook. It's a nice area."

Cynthia looked dreamy-eyed. "Yeah, I bet it is. I've always thought it would be the perfect place to live."

"It is pretty. My house is in the village." He spent little time there so he hadn't given his surroundings much thought. When he'd moved to town, one of the other doctors had told him that he should consider living in the area so he had.

"Really? Nice."

Apparently he'd impressed her. He certainly hadn't with the amount of fun he had. What was her deal with fun anyway? "See, I live in Mountain Brook and ride a bike so I can have fun."

"I didn't mean to imply that you couldn't."

He gave her his best hurt look. "I think that's exactly what you intended to do."

"I did not!" Cynthia looked indignant.

"You were making fun of me for not having fun." He laughed when she stuck out her tongue at him. "That's the best you have for a comeback? Second-grade gestures? I'll always win our arguments if you can't do any better than that."

Cynthia loved his full-bodied laugh almost as much as she did listening to him speak. The man could be charming and frustrating. But she had to admit she was enjoying their conversation immensely. What would it be like to have him at her kitchen table like this all the time? She shouldn't think that way. It wasn't going to happen.

Digging the spoon into the ice cream, she scooped a large amount and placed it on his plate.

"You're being very free with that," Sean said, observing his plate.

"I don't know any male who doesn't like his

ice cream. It was my father's favorite. Said you could never have too much."

"Well, he might have been right about that but it's easy to get fat on." Sean picked up a smaller spoon she'd laid nearby.

Cynthia took a moment to let her look roam over his trim, muscular physique. "Oh, I think you'll be all right."

"Why, Ms. Marcum, I think you just checked me out." He gave her a teasing grin.

"Dr. Donavon, don't let it go to your head." His eyes widened at her remark and a slow wolfish grin formed on his lips.

Only then did she comprehend the double meaning. With a gulp, she realized what she'd said. Heat rushed to her cheeks. She snatched the top of the ice cream off the table, replaced it and headed for the refrigerator.

"You don't want any ice cream?" he asked with a soft chuckle.

"I don't need any."

His voice went lower. "If you keep talking dirty to me I'll need some more and a cold shower to boot."

Cynthia pulled the freezer door wide, trying

to hide her reaction to his teasing. She couldn't spend the rest of the night with her head in the cold so she took a deep breath and pushed the door closed. This was too much. She'd fantasized about him for too long. Sexual fencing wasn't something she was prepared for.

"Are you flirting with me?" She tried to make it sound like an accusation, but it came out sounding a tad hopeful.

"I just thought you could use a little fun as well." He was watching her closely.

They were having fun. The type she'd not shared with a man in a long time, if ever. Dave was a rather dry person with no quick wit. She rather liked flirting.

Cynthia watched as Sean put a spoon full of ice cream in his mouth. He had such a beautiful one. A full lower lip with a thinner upper one, not too wide, and very masculine. She would call it kissable.

Ideas like that had to stop. They were becoming too frequent and too disturbing. Just because Sean had been going to kiss her in the elevator didn't mean he still wanted to. Squaring her shoulders, Cynthia controlled the shaking of her knees. She sat, leaving plenty of space between them.

"You know, it has been a long time since I've been to a birthday party." He took a bite of cake.

"Really? Even for your family?"

Sean felt her full attention on him. She obviously thought everyone saw family in the same way. He shook his head. "No. I don't get together with my family much."

"Why not? They live far away?" She studied him as if he were some strange lab specimen.

"Not really. Only a couple of hours."

"I can't imagine not seeing my brothers every day." She ate some more cake.

"I haven't seen my brother or sister in a couple of years. We're just not a close family. Do you think your brothers will always live right here or close by? They could move away."

"I know that. But we would always visit." She paused as if she wasn't sure she should say more before asking, "Did something happen in your family that causes you not to go see them?"

"Yeah. I got away." He hoped he made it clear by his tone he wanted to change the subject.

"Oh." Cynthia returned her attention to her plate.

It wasn't Cynthia's business what went on with his family. He didn't like talking about them. How he felt. It didn't matter anyway. He was his own man now. Not involved with people who thought or acted as his parents did.

"I'm sorry. I've been nosey. Very rude of me. My brothers accuse me of that all the time."

Sean forced a smile. "Let's just say my childhood doesn't hold my fondest memories."

They ate quietly for a few minutes.

"What does hold your fondest memories?"

"More questions." He gave her a pointed look. She acted as if she wanted to apologize again but he continued. "Playing paintball will now be one. I rather enjoyed the part where I shot the boy overtaking us while you were under me."

Cynthia gave him a searching look while seeming to dare him at the same time. "Are you flirting with me again?"

"What if I was?" Somehow her answer was going to mean more than it should. He really liked her. Respected the confidence with which she faced him head-on.

She looked away. "I'm not sure I want to answer that question."

Maybe she was feeling the same about him as he was her. He grinned. "I think you already have." Sean placed his spoon on the empty plate. Now he needed to give her room to think about that. "I really should be going."

"I'm sorry you got caught up in my family craziness."

"No big deal." He shrugged a shoulder. "I was glad I was around to help." When he got to his feet Cynthia did too. She followed him to her front door. Opening it, he turned back to her. "You know, I don't think I can leave until I've finished what I started. I wouldn't be able to sleep."

Her perplexed expression brought a smile to his face.

Placing a finger under her chin, he lifted it. "This." He placed his mouth on hers. Her lips tasted amazing, just as he'd thought they might. They were plump, soft and sweet from the icing. When she didn't resist he stepped closer, taking the kiss deeper.

Her hands rested on his waist.

"Hey, Cyn." Rick's voice carried from the direction of the kitchen.

She pulled back and studied Sean with charmingly dazed eyes, making him want to kiss her on the way to the nearest bedroom.

He said softly, "The next time I kiss you I'm going to make sure we can't be interrupted." As Rick came around the corner Sean said in a normal tone, "Good night, Cynthia."

The next morning Cynthia was still reliving, basking in, the pleasure of Sean's lips touching hers. Yet, she still wondered what it meant. Could he be interested in a real relationship or was he just playing with her? Not that she hadn't enjoyed it. To the contrary, she had very much. They really didn't have anything in common except that she did his transcription. Yet they seemed to have a good time together. Even laughed a couple of times. But he wasn't into family. He'd said so.

She only had time for her family right now. More than that, she wanted a husband and children. Forever. But, was that what he was looking for?

Despite all the questions and the push-pull between them, she'd savored his kiss. Found it too brief. Wanted another. Had she daydreamed about him for so long, built him up in her mind to the point it would be impossible for him to meet her expectations? Yet, she found the real Sean Donavon even more fascinating than the fantasy. It had taken nothing but a simple kiss to make her envision being wrapped in his arms, pressed against his chest and thoroughly loved. Her imagination was already warping into overdrive. She laughed. In reality he probably kissed everyone who offered him ice cream.

By midmorning she had checked her emails four times more than usual but still found no notes from Sean. What had she expected? He had a busy practice and was working on the grant. She was being silly. He didn't have time to waste typing emails to her all the time. Still she looked for one.

Disgusted with herself and determined to get him off her mind, she finished transcribing work for another doctor and called Ann Marie's house to check on her. Her mother was civil but only gave her a short statement that Ann Marie was doing fine and had gone to school on crutches. She also said that Dr. Donavon had called and it wasn't necessary that she do so as well.

Cynthia was still glad she had made the effort. Despite how irresponsible Ann Marie's mother thought she might be, Cynthia still took her responsibility as the adult in the family seriously. She'd found the high road and done the right thing by checking on the girl. It had been nice to have Sean's support the night before. Sometimes holding down the parent position in her family was a heavy burden. At the hospital had been one of those times. Taking on major adult duties under difficult circumstances hadn't been easy.

Right now what she should do was concentrate on the transcription she needed to finish. By the middle of the afternoon a message popped into the system that Sean had submitted some dictation. She was down to typing nothing but those an hour later. She'd always left his work for last but now that she'd been kissed by him the thought of his voice in her ear was almost too sensual, too personal.

Left no choice, she opened his material, replaced her headphones and clicked on the first report. With her fingers on the keyboard and prepared for Sean's voice, she still hadn't expected the jolt she received when he said, "Hello, Cynthia."

Her heart did a little tap dance. She almost melted in the chair. Leaning back in her chair, she closed her eyes, basking in the timbre of his voice.

"I hope you're having a good day."

I am now.

"When you finish the dictation on this tape would you mind printing them and letting the office know? I need them right away. By the way, I enjoyed yesterday evening. Maybe we could do it again sometime soon."

How was she supposed to concentrate after that? This had to stop. Her obsession with the man. But still a girl could dream. Could bask in it until it ended. And it would end, she was sure.

Straightening in the chair, Cynthia pressed her lips together. It was time for her to get serious. As if that would happen while Sean was speaking in her ear. Still, this was work that must be completed. He needed it. She needed the paycheck.

For the next hour, she barely managed to stay focused on what Sean was saying and not on how her body was reacting to his voice. It was almost a relief to finish the last report. The business day was almost over when she typed the last word. She called Sean's office and was told by the office manager that it was too late for a messenger service to come.

"Then I'll just bring them in," she told the woman.

"I'm sure that Dr. Donavon will appreciate that."

Cynthia took a few moments to wash her face, brush her hair and change clothes before she headed out of the door. The trip back to her house from downtown wouldn't be enjoyable during rush hour but Sean had said he needed the reports. She refused to let herself contemplate the little thrill she felt over just having a chance to see Sean again.

Would he be glad to see her?

Pulling into his office parking lot a few minutes before closing time, Cynthia headed into the building. The receptionist was still behind the window but obviously preparing to leave.

"I have some transcription that Sean, uh…Dr. Donavon requested for today."

At her use of his first name the woman's head jerked up and her eyes filled with interest. The receptionist looked her over as if she'd never really given her any thought the other times they'd met. Once again, she seemed to dismiss her as unimportant. Apparently she didn't see Cynthia as competition material.

Raising her nose slightly, the woman said, "Dr. Donavon is with a patient."

Disappointment filled Cynthia but this trip wasn't about her cow-eyed crush on Sean. Cynthia handed the packet of reports to the woman. "I understand. I don't need to disturb him. Please make sure he gets these reports right away."

The woman nodded and went back to what she had been doing.

Cynthia refused to look down the hallway in the direction of Sean's office as she made her way out of the lobby. She was in her car buckling in when there was a rap on the driver's side window. Her heart jumped in her chest as she jerked around. Sean stood there.

He indicated for her to roll the window down.

When she did he said as if disappointed, "You weren't going to say hi?"

Her pulse raced from her excitement at seeing him. "I was told you were seeing a patient."

"You could have waited." He sounded disappointed. Leaning down so his face was in the window, he said, "Are you hungry?"

He was close. So very close. What would he say if she traced his lips with her finger? "Hungry?" Absorbed in thinking about his lips, she wasn't really listening.

"Yes. Hungry. You know, food, stomach making noises. Five o'clock somewhere."

Cynthia blinked and came back to the real world. The man had put a spell on her, turning her brain to mush whenever he was around. "I know what it is. I just wasn't sure why you were asking."

He grinned. One of those "nice guys in wolf's clothing" kind. The type where a girl should run but couldn't because she was afraid that she might regret it. "I wanted to see if you'd like to grab some dinner with me. I missed lunch. My surgery case went longer than expected."

Cynthia tingled all over. Sean was asking her to dinner. "I guess I could be interested in dinner."

He chuckled. "You're not going to dare act as if you might like me, are you?"

Cynthia gave him a syrupy smile. She had to play it cool. Not let on how keen she was on the idea. That was the problem: she liked him too well. So much so, she could be swept away by him. "I have a feeling that if you had the upper hand you'd take advantage of it. Then I'd be in big trouble."

Sean leaned in closer. His face inches from hers. "You know, Cynthia, sometimes it's fun to live dangerously. You do believe in fun, don't you?"

She did. Danger she wasn't so sure about. Her heart wasn't something she played with. And she had no idea where all of this was going. It took her a moment to answer. "I do. But I also need to know I won't get hurt while I'm having fun."

"It's just supper, not a long-term contract," he said softly.

Cynthia took a moment to give that some thought. She wanted to go so why was she holding back? There hadn't been a man in her life in a long time and now a nice one wanted to take her out. Why wouldn't she take a chance? "I guess I could. I'd have to sit in traffic at this hour to get home anyway."

He straightened a little, just missing the top of the door. "So what you're saying is that sharing a meal with me is just a step better than sitting in traffic."

She smiled. "Now you're trying to put words in my mouth."

"So what'll it be? Me or the traffic?" His eyes dared her to agree.

Truthfully it wasn't a hard decision. Sean would win every time. "I'll have supper with you."

He grinned and gave the door a thump with his palm. "Great. Come on back inside and we'll go in my car. I'll drop you back here when we're done."

Sean waited while she rolled up the window, got out and locked the car. Together they walked back to his office building.

For once Cynthia wished she'd taken more time with her appearance. It had been so long since she'd been on a date the idea seemed almost foreign. Still, she could hardly contain the anticipation bubbling up because Sean had gone to the effort to catch her before she'd left the parking lot.

His receptionist's eyes widened then narrowed as they walked past her. Cynthia was tempted to give her a gloating smile but didn't.

In his office Sean went behind his desk and removed his lab coat, draping it over the back of his chair.

"I don't think your receptionist likes me. I just got the evil eye. Methinks there's a story there." Cynthia studied him. She wouldn't appreciate being a part of Sean's harem.

Sean glanced up from the papers he was putting into a stack on his desk. "Nothing you should be worried about."

"I don't need to step in the middle of something." She had enough complications in her life. Didn't need to get involved with a womanizer. Her heart had been broken once and she had no interest in having that repeated.

Sean stopped what he was doing and came around the desk. "To put your mind at ease we went out a couple of times. As friends."

Cynthia angled her head at an angle and gave him a skeptical look.

He quirked his mouth. "Okay. I thought friends. She wanted more."

"So what do you want from me?" Cynthia was rethinking going to dinner. Maybe they should just remain employee and employer. She needed this job, no heartache. He already had the ability to give her that. Was she willing to take that chance? To have him disrupt her ordered life?

Sean moved closer, not into her personal space but near enough to take one of her hands. "Friends, at least. More, I hope. Look, I've already discussed and explained more in order to get you to go out to dinner with me than I have with any other woman. Trust me. Let's just get to know each other and see what happens."

Maybe it was time for her to stop worrying all the time and have some fun for a change. After all, she was the one who believed in it. "Okay."

"Great. Let's go." He smiled and let her step out of the door ahead of him.

Sean directed her down the hall to the back of the building. As they passed his nurse he said good night and asked her to see that the office was secure.

Running through a slow but steady rain, they quickly climbed into his car. Cynthia laughed and pushed at her hair as if trying to put it into some sort of order. He rather liked her less polished look. The tight-skirt, glossy-lipped, shiny-jewelry-adorned women paled in comparison to Cynthia's fresh-faced, meet-life-head-on personality. It had an appeal that pulled at him. "There's a nice place not far from here where we can get a good meal."

"Sounds perfect. You know your car isn't at all what I pictured you driving," Cynthia said as she buckled up.

He gave her a questioning look. "How's that?"

"I don't know. I always pictured you as a sports car kind of guy."

She had been imagining him? "Where did you get that idea?"

"Your voice." She looked out of the windshield instead of at him as if she'd said more than she had intended to.

"My voice? I didn't know you could tell what kind of car a person would buy by their voice.

Is that a new medical discovery?" He started the car.

Cynthia looked at him. "No. More like dream therapy."

Sean gave that a thoughtful nod. This conversation was getting interesting. "Been dreaming about me, have you?"

She vigorously shook her head, her hair covering her face. "No, just my overactive imagination, which had put surgeon, good practice and bachelor into an equation and come out with hot red sports car. You can tell math is not my strongest subject."

He backed out of the parking spot. "So you had me figured as a cliché. All your information may be true but you also forgot to figure in loans for medical school. And not every doctor feels the need to live extravagantly."

"I guess they don't. But I wasn't thinking that practically."

"Are you disappointed?" He waited with anticipation for her answer. For some reason it would hurt if she was.

"No. I'm not so shallow as to base my friendship with someone on the type of car he drives."

"That's encouraging to know." Sean pulled out into the street, a sense of relief washing over him. He wouldn't be interested in any woman who was only concerned about how much was in his wallet. As far as he was concerned that was another get rich scheme. More than one woman had thought he was their way to the good life. The latest being his receptionist.

"I know what you mean."

He glanced at her. "That sounds like there's a little bitterness in that statement."

A soft contrite sigh came from her. "I guess there is."

"Despite being a surgeon whose patients are asleep during most of his interaction with them, I'm a good listener." He really wanted to know what was behind her reaction. Somehow he believed it had something to do with Cynthia's hesitancy at them becoming more than doctor and transcriptionist.

"I had a boyfriend. It was pretty serious. We were talking about getting married, then my parents died. I had my brothers to be concerned about. It wasn't long before he'd had enough and was gone."

"That must have been tough." If nothing else the timing was poor. When she'd needed support the most she'd been let down. No wonder she was so suspicious of his actions. But even if they started dating he didn't see their relationship becoming too involved. He wouldn't be around long enough for her to depend on him.

"Yeah, it was," she said in a flat tone.

They were quiet for a few moments as he worked his way through traffic.

Suddenly Cynthia cried, "Oh, no. You've got to take me back to my car."

"What? Why?" Had she forgotten something? Was she in pain?

"I forgot about Rick's game tonight. I've never done that before." She pulled out her phone. "I can just make it if I hurry."

Sean was relieved that it wasn't something serious. "Doesn't he have other games he'll play?" Why was her seeing a basketball game so important?

"This is his senior year. I've not missed one." She looked around anxiously as if she was in a panic to get to her car.

"Surely you have time for a quick dinner?

We're almost to the restaurant." He'd gone to such effort to convince her to eat with him. He couldn't help being disappointed she'd rather go to a high-school basketball game instead of spending time with him.

"I'm sorry but I really must go. Rick expects me to be there. He has no one in the stands to support him if I'm not. Don't you remember how important it was to have someone rooting for you?"

He couldn't. The few times his parents had had the money to let him be a part of an after-school activity they hadn't ever shown up to see him participate. They had always been having meetings to get people to join their various business ventures. There hadn't been time to watch him play ball. If they had attended they'd spent their time trying to recruit people to join them. No, he knew nothing about the support Cynthia was talking about.

"No. My parents weren't very good at that sort of thing," he said in a neutral tone.

She looked at him for a moment before quietly saying, "I'm sorry. Supporting each other is what my family does. No matter how small the event. I have to go. Rick will worry if I'm not there."

Twisting in his direction, she added, "Sean, I'm truly sorry for bailing at the last minute." Briefly she touched his arm. "Hey, why don't you come to the game with me? I can get your dinner." She smiled. "Hotdog, fries and popcorn."

"As appetizing as that sounds, I've got to work tonight." The food didn't sound that appealing but he sure would miss spending time with her.

She waved a hand. "I need to make up for running out on you. How about coming to dinner Sunday night?"

He shook his head. "I wish I could but I have this grant hanging over my head."

"Bring the work with you and we'll spread it out on the table, look at it on the laptop. I'll see what I can do to help you. I've done enough of the reports for it that I think I have an idea of where you're headed."

"I don't know." Still, he was tempted. He wanted to get to know her better and she was offering help he needed. Maybe he could accomplish two things at once.

"You're afraid I'm a bad cook, aren't you?" Cynthia's look was piercing.

He grinned. "Well, maybe a little."

"I'll tell you what, if you don't like my cooking… I don't know what I'll do. But I do wish you'd come to dinner. I feel horrible about this."

Her eyes were begging him to agree. "It's not necessary but a home-cooked meal does sound appealing. Okay. And I'll bring work along. I'm not going to turn down good help."

After he'd heard her story about her ex he was sure he would lose any chance he had with her if he didn't take this in his stride. A few minutes later he pulled up next to her car.

A broad smile lit Cynthia's face and she planted a quick kiss on his cheek. When she pulled back she appeared shocked. Hurrying out of his car, she said in a rush, "Great. I'll see you at seven."

Sean watched as she pulled out of the lot. He couldn't deny feeling put out at her dropping him to go to her brother's game. Nothing in him or his background gave him a basis to comprehend that type of devotion. Still, he had to respect her commitment to her brothers even if he thought it was a little over the top. What would it be like to have someone care about him with such devotion?

CHAPTER FIVE

TWO EVENINGS LATER Sean showed up at Cynthia's house right at seven. To avoid looking too eager, he arrived on time even though he'd been looking forward to her dinner all day. He'd spent more time anticipating his date with her than he had on the looming grant deadline.

There was still so much to organize. He hoped Cynthia would be able to make sense of the tangle of information he was trying to get in order. After asking her to help him he realized that he didn't even know where to have her start. All he knew to do was bring what he had and let her have at it. With the deadline looming he was afraid he would be putting in several long days ahead.

That afternoon he'd sent her an email.

Cynthia
Looking forward to dinner tonight. Can I bring something?
Sean

A few minutes later the reply had come back.

No—just yourself.
Cynthia

When was the last time he'd been interested in a girl who was equally interested in him? Not his money or position? He liked the idea that he alone was enough for Cynthia. But was that really true? He didn't know her well enough to state that as fact. Still, the idea it could be true made him feel something he hadn't in a long time. Wanted.

The porch light was on and the house looked welcoming. He'd become so used to going home to his dark house that the idea someone was expecting him pleased him. He climbed a couple of steps and knocked on the door. Seconds later it was slung open by a younger man who Sean hadn't met before. He surmised that the man must be Cynthia's middle brother, Mark. Sean suppressed his disappointment that Mark wasn't Cynthia. It would have been nice to have a chance at another kiss.

"Hey, man, you must be Sean. I'm Mark. Come on in," Mark offered. Sean stepped inside. “Cyn’s in the kitchen buzzing around. You must be a pretty big deal. I haven’t seen her this excited since her prom night.” Mark pushed the door closed with a slap.

He headed down the hall and Sean followed. So Cynthia was acting out of character because of him. Interesting.

An amazing smell wafted to his nose. If he had to guess it was roast beef. His stomach reacted to the pull of his favorite meal. His mother used to fix it on his birthday. It didn’t matter if they were in dire straits at the time or not, she saw to it each of her children got their favorite meal on their birthdays. He had all but forgotten about that.

Mark passed the kitchen entrance and continued down the hall. Cynthia turned away from the sink and smiled when he entered the kitchen. Sean returned the smile as he set down his bag with the grant material in it. If he got that kind of welcome every time he went home, he wouldn’t spend nearly as much time at the office.

“Hey.” There was a touch of pink on her cheeks.

“Hi. I did as you said. I came empty-handed.” He stepped closer, looking over her shoulder.

"That's what you were supposed to do." There was a little nervous wobble in her voice. Tomatoes, lettuce and a cucumber sat in the sink.

"What're you up to?"

She looked at him. "I'm surprised that a man of your intelligence wouldn't recognize salad fixin'."

"There you go starting with the smart mouth. You should be careful about talking to me like that. I might not offer my help." When had he ever teased a woman in the kitchen? When had a woman he was going out with offered to prepare him dinner? In the short time he'd known Cynthia he'd experienced a number of personal firsts.

"Since you offered to help..." She stepped back, bumping into him.

Sean reached for her but she scooted away. Opening a drawer, she withdrew a small cutting board. "How about you slicing the tomato and cucumber?"

It had been some time since he'd helped in the kitchen but he was game if it meant being around Cynthia. "I can do that."

She handed the board to him and pulled a knife

out of a wooden block on the counter. "Here you go. I'm going to check on the roast. It should be almost done."

Sean picked up a tomato. Placing it on the board, he sliced it. He wasn't about to let on that he didn't know what he was doing. Cynthia opened the oven and the aroma made his stomach growl. The sooner he had this salad finished, the sooner they could eat. As he continued to chop she set the table.

"Here's a bowl for that." Cynthia set a glass one on the counter next to him, then she flitted away again.

"Thanks." Sean continued to chop. He felt surprisingly comfortable spending time on something as domestic as preparing a meal. It had been so long since he'd been in a home where that was done. Really since he had left his parents as an eighteen-year-old. For some reason he was thinking of them far more often after meeting Cynthia and her brothers.

A few minutes later she asked, "Are you about done there?"

"I didn't know I had a time limit. Damn!" Sean

jerked his hand back. Looking down, he saw blood dripping from the end of his thumb.

Cynthia was at his side instantly. "What've you done? Let me see." She snatched a dish towel off a hook attached to the cabinet. Wrapping her hand around his wrist, she raised it above his heart and covered his thumb with the towel.

His finger throbbed with every beat of his heart and his stomach roiled. This sort of cut was far worse pain-wise than the type he made in surgery.

"You look a little green," Cynthia said. "Come over here and sit down." She led him to a chair at the table, still holding his hand in the air.

Sean gladly sat.

"Mark," Cynthia called, urgency evident in her voice.

Seconds later there was the sound of feet hurrying down the hall. Mark came into the kitchen.

"Get me the first-aid kit out from under the sink in my bath," she instructed.

"What happened?" he asked, sounding concerned.

She lifted the towel and looked at the thumb. "Sean cut himself. Now go."

Mark left.

Cynthia turned back to Sean. “I need to look at this and see how bad it is. You may need stitches.”

Sean winced as she finished removing the rag and air hit the wound. He watched her face as she studied his thumb. Her nose wrinkled up and her lips drew into a tight line. “Who would have thought a surgeon wouldn’t be able to handle a knife?” There was a note of humor in her tone but she said it with a straight face.

That remark didn’t make him feel any better. “Is that your best bedside manner?”

She recovered his finger and looked at him, saying sweetly, “I’m sorry. Does it hurt terribly?”

His look met hers. “Actually, at the risk of sounding less than manly, it does.”

“I’m sorry.” Compassion covered her face and she placed a hand on his shoulder. “I’ll get you cleaned up and you should be fine. It’s not too deep or long.” Her attention turned to Mark as he put the first-aid box on the table then left. “Thanks,” she called. To Sean she said, “I want you to apply pressure here while I wet some gauze to clean you up."

"You do realize I'm a doctor, don't you?" At least with her so close he was starting to think about other things than the throbbing of his thumb.

"Right now you're my patient." She opened the box and pulled out a couple of packages of square gauze. Tearing the paper, she removed them, dropping the covering on the table. "Come over to the sink." She moved there and ran water over the gauze. He joined her. She handed him the square that had been folded in half. "You hold this."

Sean took it and watched as she removed the towel. Carefully she cleaned around the injury.

"At least it doesn't require stitches." She sounded satisfied. "I'll disinfect it and bandage it well. You should be fine." Cynthia met his look. "This won't prevent you from doing surgery, will it?"

He shook his head. "No. I'm not scheduled until the day after tomorrow and it should be healing well by then."

"Good." She truly seemed relieved. "I'd hate

for you to have to move your surgery schedule around because I had you making a salad. Put that gauze over the opening and go back to the table. I'm going to get the roast out so we don't have a fire on top of a cut hand. I'll cover that in just a sec."

Sean returned to his chair, glad his stomach had settled. He was embarrassed enough; if he'd passed out it would've been worse. He didn't mind other people's blood but had never liked the sight of his own.

Cynthia was beside him seconds later. Using a Betadine swab, she cleaned around the cut, applied an antibacterial ointment and placed a clean gauze pad over the area and taped it.

Impressed, he remarked, "You're really quite good at this. When do you plan to return to school? Good nurses are always needed."

"I've got to see the boys get through school and are on their way." She didn't slow down as she spoke.

Sean looked at the top of her head in disbelief. "Boys? They're young men, you know. I think you underestimate them."

"You don't understand." By her tone she was firmly dismissing the subject.

He didn't understand. It was as if she was hiding behind her brothers. Didn't want to move on. Wasn't accepting her parents had died. That her brothers were growing out of needing her attention all the time. That she had a life too that she should be living.

Cynthia cleaned up the first-aid kit and pushed it aside. She smiled at him. "Now, if you're through creating pre-dinner drama I'll get our food on the table."

Sean smiled weakly. "Please don't let me stand in the way. I'm hungry and that roast smells wonderful. I'll finish the salad."

She put a hand on his shoulder when he started to stand. "You stay right there. I'll do it. By the way, I saw that green look on your face. Was that the look of a surgeon who doesn't like the sight of blood?"

"Thanks for making an already embarrassing situation even more so," he grumbled. "Actually other people's blood doesn't bother me, just my own."

She grinned. "Your secret is safe with me."

"Cyn, when are we going to eat?" Rick asked from the doorway.

"In just a few minutes. Help me get everything on the table," Cynthia said without slowing her movements.

Just minutes later Mark joined them. "How's the finger?"

"I'll live," Sean said as he turned in his chair and put his leg beneath the table. He wouldn't admit that it was still throbbing.

Rick came to sit beside him. Mark helped put bowls of food on the table and took a chair, leaving the one closest to Sean for Cynthia. Soon she slipped into it.

Sean didn't want to count the number of years it had been since he'd sat at a kitchen table and had a family meal. Cynthia said a short prayer then said to him, "Hand me your plate and I'll serve you. It's too hot and heavy to pass."

Cynthia filled his plate with meat, potatoes, carrots and onions and handed the plate back to him. She did the same for her brothers.

"Rick, pass that corn around." She picked up the rolls and offered them to Sean.

He took one and passed the dish along. Not until everyone had a full plate did Cynthia pick up her fork and start eating. Was she always seeing about everyone else? Sean had never seen a less self-centered person.

Sean couldn't believe how wonderful the tender roast tasted as well as the other food. Despite his earlier stomach distress, he loved the meal. He'd been missing a part of life he hadn't realized he'd lost. "Mmm. This is the best."

"Thanks. I'm glad you think so." Cynthia smiled at him. "The meat came from an internet mail-order company. I think it's excellent quality. I have a friend who sells it. She wants me to join the company. To make money or get free products all I have to do is to get others to join. That shouldn't be too hard. The product sells itself."

Sean flinched and almost choked on his food. Where had he heard those words before? They sounded suspiciously like something his parents would be involved in. Just another get-rich-quick scheme. He didn't want to have anything to do with that type of thing. Or someone who was doing it. He worked to keep his voice even. How was he going to comment? He couldn't say: why would you want to do that? He settled on, "I'm not a fan of those types of deals."

Cynthia gave him an inquiring look. "Why's that?"

"Because they often don't pan out as advertised. It also takes time to get people to join. I would think you have enough going on."

"If the money was good I would make time. I think it'd be easy enough to sell. The food is good." Cynthia took a forkful of corn. "Would you like to be my first customer?" She looked at him. "Sign up under me?"

How was he going to answer that question nicely? There was no way he would get involved even for her. "No, thank you. I don't eat at home enough to make it worth my while."

"I guess your lifestyle doesn't lend itself to cooking much."

Somehow that made him sound sort of sad. "Maybe what I need to do is just come here more often." Sean smiled at her, then her brothers.

She looked directly at him. "Maybe we can work something out."

Sean glanced at her brothers to find them grinning and elbowing each other. They were enjoying his and Cynthia's exchange. "So, Rick, how's the basketball going?"

The teen almost choked on his drink he had just picked up. "Pretty good. I think we have a real chance to make the playoffs this year."

"That sounds great. And have you seen Ann Marie?" Sean asked.

Rick's face took on a red tint before he looked down at his plate.

"Isn't that the girl that got hurt at your birthday party?" Mark asked, looking to all of them for an answer.

"Yes. But she isn't just some girl," Rick said, pointing his fork at his brother.

Mark gave him a teasing look and said in a singsong voice, "Rick's got a girlfriend."

"Shut up, Mark. You're just jealous no one'll look at your ugly mug," Rick snapped back.

"Boys, that's enough. Sean doesn't want to hear all that," Cynthia said, as if she refereed regularly.

Cynthia really did act as if she were the boys' parent instead of their sister. Couldn't she see they were all grown up? Or was she afraid to let go? Sean said, “I don’t mind. My older brother treated me the same way.”

They all quieted as they continued eating their meal. Mark’s phone rang and he picked it up.

“You know there are no phones at meals,” Cynthia said as he touched the screen to answer.

“I need to get this. It might be about a new job I applied for today.” He slid out of the chair.

Cynthia didn’t look pleased as she watched Mark leave the room.

Minutes later he returned with excitement written all over his face and pumping the air. “I got the job. I got the job.” He slid into the chair again, almost vibrating with excitement. “It’s full time. I’m going to be working at Action Auto.”

“That’s great, but won’t that be hard to handle with school?” Cynthia asked.

Sean gave her a speculative look. Wasn’t she glad he had gotten a job? It looked as if she would appreciate his help with the finances. Sean had been brought up in a household where anyone who had a steady job was unusual. Except for him. He’d handled work and school. Had been the first to take on a job when he'd been old enough. It was something that his parents couldn't do. Cynthia should be proud of Mark.

"I told you I wasn't going back to school next semester," Mark almost snarled.

"Mama and Daddy wanted you to go to school," Cynthia insisted.

Mark leaned across the table. "They're not here. And they wanted you to go too."

Cynthia appeared stricken. "We should honor their wishes. You know I plan to go back."

"Then you go instead of me. For right now I'm going to work." Mark pushed his chair back and stood. "I've got to get things together for tomorrow. Thanks for dinner."

Sean hurt for Cynthia, could see her unhappiness. As if her world were dissolving around her.

She looked at him. "I'm sorry, Sean. This isn't how we were raised to treat a guest."

"It's okay. Dinner and entertainment. That's more than I usually have on a Sunday evening. I'm not complaining."

That got a ghost of a smile out of her. "Thanks for understanding."

Rick's chair screeched as he pushed it back. "I've got a project to work on. See y'all later."

Sean looked at Cynthia and smiled. "I guess that leaves us doing the dishes."

"I'm sorry the evening turned into a family feud. It seems that I'll owe you another meal to make up for this one." Cynthia rose from the table.

"That works out perfectly for me. How about dinner Friday night? I'll pick you up at seven." Sean wasn't sure about Cynthia being involved in a selling pyramid scheme or her over-devotion to her brothers, but he couldn't resist getting to know her better. Regardless of their differences, he found her interesting and sincere. He just plain old-fashioned liked her. It wasn't as if they'd ever become involved enough to marry but he did like her company.

Cynthia carried the roast beef platter to the kitchen counter. "I'm supposed to be the one doing a meal for you."

"Next time. This time I want to take you out." Sean picked up two bowls and followed her to the kitchen counter.

"That sounds like fun. Let me take care of

cleaning up. I don't want you to accidentally hit your thumb."

"I'm not an invalid. I can at least carry things to you." He didn't give her a chance to respond before he returned to the table and picked up a bowl. "Do Rick and Mark ever help with cleaning up? After all, you do the cooking."

She squirted dish liquid into the sink. "Not really. They have a lot going on."

"More than you? I'd think the three people could split the work three ways," Sean commented as he added another plate to the dishwasher.

Tension filled the air between them. Had he said too much? Sounded too critical?

Cynthia didn't say anything and continued to clean.

"I'm sorry if I said something wrong." Sean hoped to get them back to teasing each other as they had been before dinner.

She shrugged. "It's no big deal."

Somehow Sean didn't believe that.

A quarter of an hour later they were finished cleaning and the air between them had been easy.

"So what did you bring to work on tonight?" she asked.

"Do you mind helping me with that organization we talked about earlier? I'm not feeling good about this grant application at all."

"Get your stuff. Bring it over here to the table and we'll have a look." Cynthia became all business.

Sean went after his bag that was still where he'd left it near the door. "Okay. Maybe with your help tonight I can make some real progress on this mess."

They spread the papers out across the table. Cynthia went to get her laptop from her office while he opened his. She returned and sat next to him. She smelled of home cooking, a hint of gardenia and something that could only be her scent alone.

Sean leaned just a little closer as they reviewed side by side the contents on their screens. For the next two hours they worked diligently trying to organize reports in a logical format. They were careful to make note of any missing support material.

Finally, he leaned back in his chair and stretched his arms up over his head, yawning. "I think this is in a better form than I have seen it in weeks. I owe that to you." His arm came down around her shoulders and he gave her a squeeze. "I can't thank you enough."

She looked directly at him. "I know you're going to make a big difference in many people's lives. It gives me a good feeling to be a part of that. Even in a small way."

"That's one of the things I like about you. Your concern for other people. Your help won't have been in a small way if I get that grant," he said as he stood.

"You'll get it."

He liked her vote of confidence too. Here she was supporting his work when he couldn't do the same with her thoughts on selling online food. Somehow it didn't seem right. Still, he couldn't support what he knew from experience was a bad idea. When was the last time he'd really had someone in his corner like this? He could get used to it. With a hand on her shoulder, he quickly responded, "Thanks for everything. The meal and the help. I'd better go. I have an early case in the morning."

Cynthia helped him gather the papers from the table. He put them in his bag along with his laptop. She walked him to the door.

He put his bag on the floor. "You know, I really enjoyed tonight."

"Even with all the blood and family fireworks?" She grinned at him.

"For the first time in a long time I had a meal with a real family. I know better than most that family meals can often be a little tough to live through. More than one of my family's was."

She nodded. "I appreciate your understanding."

He glanced down the hall fully expecting one of her brothers to come around the corner. Every time he attempted to kiss her they were interrupted. This time he didn't care whether someone saw them or not. "Did I say thank you for patching up my thumb?"

"You did." She looked at him with those questioning eyes. "More than once."

"But I don't think I did it properly." Sean slipped his hands around her waist and pulled her to him. She didn't back away. Instead she came to him willingly. His heart beat faster. Cynthia wanted him to kiss her. His mouth found hers warm and welcoming. She came closer, bringing her body to meet his, hands moving up to the nape of his neck. It didn't require much coaxing for her to part her lips. Her tongue shyly touched his before she joined him in the hottest kiss of his life. He pulled her tighter against him. With a moan edged with regret, she placed both her hands on his shoulders and pushed away.

Her dazed look met his, revealing she had been just as affected by their kiss as he was. "I think you need to go before we forget my brothers are just down the hall."

Her brothers. He continued to hold her and leaned his forehead against hers for a moment, struggling to get his raging libido under control. Gazing deep into her guileless eyes, he muttered, "I guess you're right. When I'm around you I forget about everything else. I'm pretty sure we shouldn't hold an X-rated show at your front door."

She gave him a sad, understanding smile and stepped back. "I would appreciate that."

"So, dinner Friday night?" Sean hoped to coax her away from he responsibilities long enough for them to find some uninterrupted time together.

"What about the grant?"

"With your help tonight I think I'm making real progress. I can take one night off. Anyway, I need to clear my head some." He ran his finger along her chin and whispered, "I think you'll make a nice distraction."

"I can't honestly say I've ever been called a distraction before." Her eyes sparkled.

His gaze didn't leave hers. "Well, if you haven't been it's the guy's problem, not yours. You're a distraction for me all the time." He gave her a quick kiss on the lips, afraid to linger any longer. "So we have a date?"

"I can't. Rick has games on Tuesdays, Fridays and Saturdays."

"Then how about Wednesday night?"

"I guess I could do that."

"I'll be here at five thirty. Wear something comfortable." Sean picked up his bag. "Thanks for the delicious meal. Good night."

CHAPTER SIX

CYNTHIA COULDN'T BELIEVE she had a date with Sean. Her life had become surreal. Never in a million years would she have guessed when she heard his sexy voice for the first time that she would be going out with him. A heavenly voice for weeks was now a flesh-and-blood man who wanted to spend time with her. She was going to make the most of it while it lasted. If nothing else she would have some great memories.

Usually all her efforts went toward the boys so she hadn't gotten a new outfit in ages but she went shopping. Sean had said casual so she had settled on a royal blue shirt and a pair of fitted dark pants that stopped just above her ankles. For shoes, she selected flats. It had been months since she'd had the money to have her hair done but she splurged and had her hair trimmed and shaped. It now bounced and flowed around her face and shoulders. With the addition of a touch of makeup to her eyes and cheeks then some gloss to her lips, she felt better than she had in years about her appearance.

She was ready to go when the doorbell rang on Wednesday evening. Resisting the urge to fling the door open, she calmly walked down the hall. Sean looked more handsome than ever. Dressed casually in a cream shirt under a wool V-necked sweater with jeans, he looked the perfect date right out of the pages of a romance novel. If she didn't get control of her infatuation she would be in trouble.

"Hey. You look incredible," he said as he stepped inside.

Warmth washed over her. She loved being complimented by him. Not many of those came from her brothers. "Thank you."

Sean lifted her chin with one finger. "You know, a blush is a rare thing of beauty. It looks good on you."

Cynthia didn't know if his statement was true but she sure enjoyed hearing it. "You don't look half bad yourself. Very dapper in a casual way."

He grinned and bowed slightly. "I do try. Are you ready to go?"

"I am. Let me just get my jacket." She turned and headed down the hall.

When she returned Sean looked over her shoulder. "Are the guys around?"

"Nope. Rick is at some friends' and Mark is at his new job. Why? Do you need them for something?"

He stepped closer and her pulse rate zipped into high gear. "I just wanted to know if we were alone." He gathered her into his arms and his lips found hers. The urgency in his kiss had her body humming, racing to join him. Seconds later he released her and stepped back. "I've been thinking about that since last Sunday night and couldn't wait any longer. I think we should go before I decide to stay here and take advantage of the privacy."

Trying to catch her breath, she said, "I guess we should go."

Was she ready for their relationship to go to the next level? Did she know him well enough? She certainly wanted him badly enough. Could she survive another broken heart? So caught up in her fantasy and infatuation with Sean, was she thinking straight?

What she did affected her brothers as well. They seemed to like him. Did they mind her having a boyfriend? Would they be hurt if she and Sean were to break up? Her brothers had already lost so much. What if they became attached to Sean? If she had the power she wouldn't let anyone hurt Mark and Rick again. She had to be careful for all their sakes who came into their lives.

Sean held the car door open while she got in before he went around and slipped gracefully into the driver's seat.

"So what do you have planned for tonight? I hope I'm dressed properly."

He looked her over as if he were feasting on the most wonderful meal of his life. "You know you look beautiful."

Cynthia warmed under his appreciation.

Backing out of the drive, he added, "I thought we would see if we could find a good view of the city. Maybe watch the lights go on. Then have a little dinner."

"That sounds wonderful." Anything she did

with Sean appealed to her. She enjoyed his humor, appreciated his devotion to his patients and his profession, but most of all she liked that he made her feel as if she were the center of his world. She'd not had that since her parents had died. As a sister or a stand-in parent, or just as the person who had to make sure everything was done, she had had little me-time in years. She'd never thought it a burden but on occasions the need to let go had nagged at her. Tonight, she planned to do just that, and with an amazing man by her side.

She found Sean's inability to organize and his rather economical way of living endearing. The smart, sexy, intelligent man had a foible. It was nice to know the perfect man she'd assembled in her mind was human. She could relate to that person.

As Sean made his way through traffic and up the mountain highway Cynthia watched as the statue of Vulcan grew larger. The huge iron man stood on the highest point in the city. She had always been fascinated by him. He was a major landmark in Birmingham and had been for all her life. It was a central mark by which people distinguished where they lived. North or south of Vulcan.

Sean continued winding around the mountain until he turned off the main highway and drove up Red Mountain to where Vulcan stood.

"This is a great place for a view of the city, but isn't it closed?" she asked.

"It is. But I have a patient who's a security guard here. I called in a favor. He's going to let us go up and have a look." Sean pulled into a parking spot in the almost deserted lot. The only vehicle there was a small older-model pickup truck.

"That sounds great." Cynthia should have known that Sean wouldn't plan a typical night out. "Once again you have surprised me."

"How's that?" Sean helped her out of the car. He lingered over letting her hand go, giving her a fuzzy feeling of pleasure.

"I thought you were the kind of guy who would take a date to a fancy restaurant. Show her how suave you are."

"Are you disappointed?" He sounded as if her answer really mattered.

Cynthia smiled. She liked the element of the unexpected he offered. “Not in the least.”

An older man with tufts of white hair on his head, wearing a gray uniform, walked toward them.

Sean shook hands with him. “Cynthia, I’d like you to meet Luther Murphy. Luther, this is Cynthia Marcum.”

The man nodded to her. “Nice to meet you, young lady. Any friend of Dr. Donavon’s is a friend of mine. Dr. Donavon did me a great service a few years back. I was getting where I couldn’t hear my wife. Most people would like that, but me, I missed hearing her complain. Dr. Donavon got me all set up so now I hear every single word she says.”

Cynthia couldn’t contain her laughter. “How long have you been happily married?”

“It’ll be forty-five years next month,” he said with a toothy grin.

“Wow, that’s impressive.” What would it be like to find a man she could love for so many years? She glanced at Sean. Could he be that one? He made her feel things she’d never experienced before. Wasn't sure she was prepared to feel again.

They walked over to a small door in the tall red-brick foundation that Vulcan stood on. Mr. Murphy opened it to reveal metal stairs that spiraled upward. He left them there.

"If we want the view we must work for it," Sean said from behind her. "Do you want me to go first?"

"No, I will." She took the lead.

Sean chuckled. "I figured as much."

She looked back at him. He was almost at eye level with her. "That's kind of like the pot calling the kettle black. You like to be in control."

"So we're going to get personal here?" He held her gaze.

"I think what I'll do is keep walking." Cynthia headed up the steps again. "Did you know that Vulcan was built for the 1904 St. Louis World Fair?"

Sean's voice echoed in the space. "Yes. Did you know that he's the largest cast-iron statue in the world?"

Pausing, she glanced back at him. "That I didn't know." She started up again. "This is a hard one. What was the point of picking a Roman god to represent Birmingham?"

"By your lofty tone you don't think I know the answer." He sounded indignant at the thought. "For your information, it was because of the area's mineral deposits. There's a large amount of iron ore in the area."

She smiled back at him. "Very good. Since you're so smart, what's Vulcan holding in his raised hand?" It took him so long to answer she began to think he might not know the answer.

"That would be a spear," he said triumphantly.

She grinned down at him. "Now for bonus points. What's in the other hand?"

A minute went by before he said, "Okay, you've got me there. What is it?"

"A hammer. It's on top of an anvil," she proudly informed him.

"That's right. Where did you get all this knowledge?" There was a little huff in his voice from the climb.

Her foot clinked as she took another step. "I did a report in the sixth grade. Got an A-plus."

Sean chuckled. "I would bring you to the one place you knew more about than me."

"Don't worry. I don't think you're less of a man for it." She stopped and waited for Sean to join her on the upper landing.

As he did he pulled her against him. "I wouldn't underestimate me there." His mouth found hers as his hand came around her waist. Her heart jumped into overdrive and she hung on as his hot and sure tongue commanded her mouth. Just as quickly he let her go, leaving her wanting more. Sean had more than proven his point.

He opened the door and stepped out onto an observation deck. She followed on shaking legs that had nothing to do with their climb. They now stood at the top of the foundation and at the feet of Vulcan.

"I haven't been here since I was a child. I have to admit I'm really looking forward to this." She looked out over the expanse of the city with awe.

Sean said, "I'm glad. I was hoping you'd like it. I wanted to do something a little different." He shook his head. "But I hadn't counted on all those steps."

"The view is worth it. Come on." She took his hand and gave it a little pull.

Sean didn't let go as they made their way

around on the narrow viewing walkway. She stopped again to look out at the panorama of the city in early evening. Only a few lights were on. Sean came to stand beside her.

"My mom and dad brought me and my brothers up here. I remember being scared and Daddy holding my hand as I made my way around. I was glued to the side of the wall until Mama took the other hand. I felt secure then." She had great memories of her parents. Missed them so much.

"You really had a great relationship with your parents, didn't you?" Sean said quietly beside her, his arm coming around her waist.

Her head leaned against his shoulder. "I did. I miss them daily."

"I don't have memories of anything like that." His tone was sad and dry.

She looked at him. He seemed troubled, as though he had said too much. "Are your parents alive?"

"Oh, they're alive and well." He gave her hand a tug. "Let's walk on around and see what downtown looks like."

"This is unreal." She looked out at the tall buildings sitting in the valley of mountains.

Sean said, "You just wait for a few more minutes and I think you'll be even more impressed."

"Is that what you're trying to do, impress me?" The fact he might care enough to try was empowering.

"Would it matter if I was?" Sean's voice had grown deeper, raspier.

She looked at him. "I do kind of like the idea."

His arm came around her waist again and they watched as darkness grew. The mountains beyond became dark silhouettes against the pink-hued sky. The sun slowly kissed them and disappeared. And lights in the city below blinked on. Some white with the occasional red and blue here and there.

"This is breathtaking," Cynthia said in awe.

"Yes, you are." She glanced at him, but he captured her look with the desire blazing in his eyes.

Cynthia swallowed hard and managed to turn back to the view. She would think about what Sean's passionate gaze and statement meant later. "How did you discover this?"

"I came up here to visit Mr. Murphy one evening and he brought me here."

She needed to keep the subject on a topic to keep her head clear. "So you make a habit of coming here?"

"No. This is the only time I've been back."

He'd never brought another woman? This was special between the two of them. She liked the idea he hadn't shared this with anyone else.

"I think it's time for us to go down and have dinner," Sean said in a low voice as they approached the doorway.

"Where're we going?" Cynthia stepped through the door and headed down the stairs.

"Do you have to know everything?" he teased.

She stiffened her shoulders and used her best annoyed voice. "Well, not everything."

"You've been looking after your brothers for so long that you need to know everything about everyone all the time. Why don't you just let go some and live a little?"

He made it sound as if she couldn't. She would show him. "This is from the man who doesn't drive a sports car, has the bare minimum in his office, and seems to work all the time." She straightened her shoulders. "I assure you I can do surprise."

He chuckled. "Ouch. That hurt. But we'll just see how well you do surprise."

They slowly descended the stairs. A few minutes later they came out of the stuffy space into the cool evening. Mr. Murphy's truck was no longer in the parking lot. Sean reached into his pocket and pulled out a small flashlight and then locked up. He directed the beam toward a path leading over a grassy slope. They walked over to it and down toward an outcropping of trees. There among them was a picnic table with a blue checked tablecloth covering it with a small candle flickering in a jar in the center. On the table sat a picnic basket.

Cynthia had never seen a more charming setting. Romantic was an understatement. She was overwhelmed with the thought he had put into their evening.

"Come on. But be careful." Sean's hand remained firmly on her elbow as he led her to the table. He helped her to sit on the bench, then went around to the other side. Opening the basket, he pulled out three plastic containers of food. A bottle of wine and two glasses followed. Another couple of containers appeared to hold slices of pie. Lastly, he removed napkins, utensils, and two plates. Sean placed a plate in front of her, then handed her a cloth napkin and a fork.

"I didn't think I could be more impressed but you've managed to do it." She was overwhelmed. He'd gone to a lot of trouble just for her.

Sean sounded pleased. "I'm glad. I was afraid my organizational skills might scare you off."

"You are worried about me being frightened off?" Why would he be afraid she wouldn't want him? From what she could tell he was almost perfect. She couldn't imagine why he might be insecure.

"A little bit," Sean was slow to admit. He took the bench across from her.

"So you put all this together all by yourself?"

"Not exactly." He started opening the plastic containers. "Truthfully, I called the local café where I often eat and they put it together." He put up a finger as if to punctuate his statement. "But I did tell them what I wanted."

Cynthia grinned. "No matter where it came

from, I can tell you went to a lot of effort. It's wonderful. I appreciate it. I'm honored."

"I'm glad you like it." He placed some fried chicken on her plate then on his. The next container held potato salad and out of the third came corn on the cob that was still warm. He brought out a small bag from the basket that had two rolls in it.

Cynthia looked at the plate before her. "This is a feast."

She glanced upward. The stars were starting to pop out and could just be seen between the limbs of the trees. The light flickering in the center of the table, the night sky and the charming man now sitting across from her were irresistible. She couldn't think of a dreamier setting.

Sean poured them each a glass of red wine and handed one to her. Hand around his goblet, he looked at her for a moment.

"Is something wrong?" she asked.

"No, I was just thinking how beautiful you looked in the candlelight."

Her heart fluttered. The man was making every effort to impress and she liked it. No man had gone to such lengths before, not even Dave.

Raising his wine for a toast, Sean said, "To an amazing woman."

Beaming, Cynthia clinked her glass to his. "Thank you. I've never been toasted before."

"Then you're long overdue." He set his glass down and waited until she started eating, then joined her. They ate in silence for a few minutes. Cynthia hated to disturb the camaraderie they had built but she couldn't get his earlier remarks about his family out of her mind. Having a support system was important. Why didn't Sean understand that?

"I hope this doesn't ruin our evening but I'm curious to know…"

"That sounds interesting and ominous at the same time." He looked up at her and put his fork down.

"What is it with you and your parents? I don't ever hear you say anything positive about them. You had a funny look on your face when we were talking about them earlier."

Sean didn't immediately answer her. Somehow he felt that the truth was all that he could share. Cynthia would see right through anything else.

Accept nothing less. He was thankful there was only candlelight for her to see him by.

"My mom and dad and I just don't think the same. I grew up with parents who see everything as pie-in-the-sky. The next great thing is coming their way. My daddy never held a solid job except for when he had no choice. They were always looking, and still are, for that get-rich-quick scheme. I'm the youngest of three. By the time they got to me there was no money. All your talk about your brothers playing basketball and doing extracurricular activities was fantasy in my childhood. Those weren't in my life because what money we had went into investing in the next thing to make us rich. Those never panned out. Not once. When I got old enough to make my own money there wasn't time for other things.

"Even on the off chance I got to do something sports related they rarely showed up. If they did come, they'd spend their time trying to recruit other parents into one of their schemes. I remember being so embarrassed.

"By the time I graduated high school we had parted ways. It was up to me to pay my way through college and I took out loans for med school. I had to do my own thing. I wanted nothing more to do with living hand to mouth. I worked in a nursing home and found I loved caring for people. I had good grades and decided that medicine was for me. Now you know all about the underbelly of my life."

Cynthia said softly, "Now I understand."

"Understand what?"

Her beautiful face was full of compassion but not pity. "Why you drive the type of car you do. Why your office looks as it does. Why you had that appalled look on your face when I wanted to sign you up for the internet meat club. Even why you picked here for our dinner."

His shoulders tensed. Did she think he should have done more for her? Just minutes ago she'd seemed impressed with what he had planned for the evening. "Are you saying you think I'm cheap?"

"No, not at all." She vigorously shook her head. "This picnic is far better than going to a fancy restaurant. I certainly have no problem with the type of car you drive. Look at what I drive. But I understand why you don't fit the cliché you accuse me of trying to force you into. Or what I expected when I first met you. All I'm saying is I get why you think the way you do."

He wasn't sure he liked being that open with another person but with Cynthia there was security. She got him and didn't dislike what she saw. He knew more than one woman who wouldn't understand or couldn't. Vulnerability wasn't his strong suite but somehow being so with Cynthia seemed right.

She tilted her head to the side. "You said you haven't seen your brother and sister in a couple of years. So how long has it been since you've seen your parents?"

"A little over a year." He was revealing stuff he'd never told anyone. He didn't talk about his family. Ever.

Disbelief covered her face. "Don't you miss them?"

"I do more since I've met your family." Again he was admitting something he normally wouldn't. How did Cynthia manage to coax information out of him?

"How's that?" She put her elbow on the table and rested her chin in her hand, studying him, leaving him no choice but to lie or to tell the truth. She would call him out if he wasn't honest. He had a feeling he would go down in her estimation if he just refused to answer.

"Being around you and your brothers at dinner just reminded me of how some of my family meals were when things were good. I didn't realize how much I had let the bad cover up everything else."

She straightened. "Thank you, I think. That must have been a tough revelation. I hope being around us isn't too painful."

It was time to talk about something besides himself. He held up his thumb. "No, except for when I cut my thumb. Oh, yeah, or when I played paintball. Those balls can cause whelps that turn into perfectly round purple bruises."

"I'm sorry. I had no idea we were so rough. I even forgot to ask about your thumb." She reached over and took his hand, caressing it.

"It's fine. I had one of the nurses re-dress it. She said whoever had done it before had done a splendid job." When she started to let go of his hand he took hers. "Tell me, what would you be doing if you weren't being a transcriptionist right now?"

"You already know. I want to be a nurse."

He gently rubbed her fingers. "So what's holding you back? Your brothers are old enough to take care of themselves."

She pulled her hand away and put both in her lap. "I need to see that Rick is settled in college. Convince Mark to go back. Then I can see about going myself."

Had he hit a nerve? Cynthia sounded defensive. Despite that he asked, "When do you think that'll happen?"

"I don't know. Maybe next year. Or the next?" She picked up her fork again.

He wanted, needed to understand her thoughts. "So what were your dreams before?"

"You mean before my parents died?" There was a sad note in her voice.

"Yes."

"I wanted to be an emergency department nurse. I liked the idea of not knowing what was going to happen next. To see all different problems. I hated it when I had to quit school." She looked off into the night. Seconds later she blinked. “You know, this discussion has gotten too serious. Who’s your favorite movie star?”

“Boy, that’s a change of subject. But I’ll go along. John Wayne.”

She nodded sagely, as if giving the idea thought. “John Wayne. I wasn’t expecting that.”

“I have his entire movie collection.”

Cynthia seemed impressed. “Really? I’ve only seen a few of his movies that I can remember.”

He leaned toward her. “I can’t believe that. How have you gotten to the age you are and seen but a few of his movies? That’s just wrong.”

“Wrong?” Her voice went up an octave and she raised her fork.

“Yes, wrong. I tell you what. We’ll finish here, go to my place to have dessert and a movie. We need to work on your education.” Sean picked up his unfinished chicken.

She shook her head. “I’m not really into Westerns.”

“I know of one I think you’ll really like.”

Cynthia smiled. “All right, I’m willing to give it a try.”

As Sean drove down the mountain he asked,

"Are you still up for a movie? I don't want to force you if you'd really rather not watch one."

"I'm still willing if I'm still invited."

As far as he was concerned she would always be invited.

All the way to Sean's house Cynthia contemplated the wisdom of agreeing to go there. It was a step in their relationship she hadn't expected. Would it just be a movie or was he hoping for more? Was she willing to give it? Having spent the last few years being cautious about men, was she prepared to open herself up to a man she'd only known for a few weeks?

What was she getting worked up over? Sean had invited her to watch a movie. He was a gentleman and wouldn't ask more than she was willing to give. That didn't make her any less nervous or ease her questions. She was crazy about him. Tonight had only intensified her fascination.

But was he interested in a real relationship? From his receptionist's reaction, he certainly was a ladies' man. But who wouldn't be interested in Sean? He was good with people, had a good sense of humor, intelligence, thought out of the box. Tonight's date proved that. Supportive. And most of all he seemed to enjoy her company. She was betting that the more she got to know him, the more she'd like him. The only thing she could find complaint with was his view of family. She couldn't understand his and he seemed to have no concept of hers. That might be an issue if they were thinking about getting married, but their relationship was nowhere near that level of involved.

Soon Sean was pulling into the driveway of a small bungalow-style house in the Mountain Brook Village area. Many of the homes appeared to have been updated, including Sean's.

"Did you do the work yourself?" she asked as she examined the woodwork detail around the door, the porch railing and light fixture. None of it looked like the typical contractor material.

"I did. I was better taking care of my fingers around the saws than I was with your knife."

This was a side of him she hadn't expected. "It looks wonderful. So you ride a bike and are good with your hands. You have an old-world talent, Doctor."

"Then I must get one more fun point."

She grinned at him. "That you do."

Now knowing his background, the choice of home, the area, and the fact he'd put more time than money into the place didn't surprise her. There wasn't a light shining on the porch. For Sean that would be a waste of money. However, when they stepped out of the car a motion light blinked on. He met her at the front of the car with the picnic basket in hand, then escorted her up a couple of cement steps to the front door. Unlocking the door, he stepped inside and flipped on a lamp.

His living area was much as Cynthia expected. Furnishings were sparse but of good quality, ones that would last. The most extravagant thing in the room was the enormous TV on the wall. She stood looking at it. "Wow."

"It was the largest I could get at the time," he said bashfully.

"Well, you certainly fit the cliché where a man and his TV are concerned." She chuckled.

"I guess I do." Sean laughed. "I have to admit that when I'm home I enjoy having it. Especially in the fall for the sports. Why don't you have a seat?" He indicated a plush-looking tan leather sofa against the opposite wall from the TV.

There was also a large matching armchair with a footstool sitting at an angle to the sofa. In front of the sofa was a coffee table with a couple of books and a few sport magazines on it in no order. There were also several books stacked in one corner. On the wall between the two front windows hung a picture of a rushing river surrounded by trees. Other than that, the room was sterile. A decorator would call it extreme minimalist. It reminded her of his office. Sean didn't waste his time or money on anything frivolous.

Yet he'd gone out of his way with dinner. So what did he consider her?

The room was definitely an extension of the man. It seemed he was so caught up in the past he couldn't let go beyond owning a large TV. How much of the extras in life was he giving up so he never felt insecure again? She bet if she accused him of being insecure he would deny it.

He'd placed his phone and keys on the coffee table along with the picnic basket. "I'll put the movie in, then get our food. We're going to watch *McLintock!*" He searched through the shelf below the TV and selected a DVD. While he put it into the machine he said, "I'll get us something to drink and the pie. What would you like? I have water, wine, soda, maybe milk." He grinned.

Taking a seat on the couch, she decided, "I'll have a soda." She was afraid to have any more alcohol, already feeling a buzz just being around Sean. With her physical reaction to him and being in his private space she couldn't afford to not be thinking straight.

As the picture came into view, he picked up the basket and left through an arched doorway. Sean returned a few minutes later with drinks in hand, then again with their pie. He took a seat in the chair; he put his feet on the stool and crossed his ankles. If she was concerned about him making an advance she shouldn't have been. Apparently, it was the last thing on his mind. Cynthia wasn't sure she liked that idea.

"Why don't you sit back and make yourself comfortable?" He took a bite of pie. "This pie is really good. You need to try yours."

Cynthia shifted until she was in the corner of the sofa. After kicking off her shoes and tucking her feet up, she ate to settle her nerves. She relaxed as she became interested in the movie. Soon her body settled, and she almost forgot Sean sitting just a few feet away.

They had been there for about fifteen minutes when he placed his plate on the table and said, "Scoot over."

She set her plate beside his and moved toward the middle of the sofa, giving him the corner space.

Sean took it. "I was lonely over there by myself."

Cynthia tried to concentrate on the movie but was so conscious of him she registered none of the words.

"Cynthia," Sean whispered.

"Mmm?" She looked at him.

"I'm still a little lonely. Why don't you come a little closer?"

A fuzzy feeling washed over her. She moved up next to him. Sean slipped his arm around her shoulders and nudged her closer.

"Now this is much better." Sean tucked her in tight.

Much. There was something nice about being

next to Sean that had nothing to do with him physically. She certainly liked his body but when she was close she felt supported, as if she wasn't facing the world alone, there was someone to share the worry. He was there. Solid. Those were feelings she shouldn't be having. He'd made no promises. It was too soon to start depending on him. She'd been let down before and she had no intention of letting that happen again. People in her life were gone too easily.

A few minutes later he whispered in her ear, "Relax, I'm not going to bite."

Cynthia snuggled up against him and rested her head in the curve of his shoulder. Here she could stay forever.

They were well into the movie when his phone rang. He paused the movie and answered. Cynthia immediately missed the warmth and comfort of him.

She couldn't help but overhear his conversation as she relished the rumble of his beautiful voice. He was soon asking questions at a swift pace. Sean had morphed into doctor mode. Apparently there had been some sort of accident. Seconds later he ended the conversation.

"I went on call at nine. I'm rarely called in during the night but tonight's one of those times. There's been an automobile accident. I'm needed at the hospital for a consult. I don't think I'll be long. I'm sorry but I don't have time to take you home. If you don't mind watching the rest of the movie I should be right back." Even though he was speaking to her she could tell that his mind was on the patient waiting.

She stood. "Don't worry about me. I know better than most that you have patients."

His hands came to her shoulders. They were warm and strong. "I know you can take care of yourself but that doesn't mean I can't worry about you. I'm sorry about running out on you. I'm not leaving without one of these."

His hands drew her to him and his lips found hers. Her arms went around his waist, pulling him tight. As his tongue requested entrance she welcomed him with a moan. Gripping her behind with both his hands, Sean brought her against him. Too quickly he released her with a groan. Cynthia teetered backwards but he held her secure. He stepped away; desire still simmered in his eyes, so intense it made her shudder.

"Now I hate to go more than ever but I'll be back soon." Sean picked up his keys and phone, and went out of the door.

Instantly his house felt huge. Cynthia had lost interest in the movie but started it again only because Sean would want to know what she thought of it. With a smile on her face, she clicked off the movie when it was over. Sean had been right: it was a good movie.

With the house quiet she carried their dirty plates and glasses to the kitchen. This space had the same charm as the rest of the house with nineteen-fifties tiles on the walls, and even appliances to match. The table was the same type she remembered her grandparents having in their kitchen. Chrome with a red top with chairs that matched. The only concession to the present day was a TV sitting on the counter. She loved the room right away. It was a perfect place to enjoy cooking a meal.

Her mother's kitchen was like that. Even after so many years she still thought of it as her mother's kitchen. Nothing had been moved or changed since her parents had died. Somehow it seemed wrong to do so. Her mother had spent so much time preparing meals there. Lots of laughter and love had been shared in that all-important space. Cynthia hadn't had the heart to make any changes. And the boys deserved for it to remain the same until they left.

She hated to think about that day fast approaching. Once again her life would drastically change.

The least she could do was wash the dishes for Sean. So caught up in musing over how much she liked his kitchen, she didn't pay close enough attention to the amount of water she was running. It backwashed out of a glass and all over her chest, soaking her, bra and all.

She was going to have to find something to wear. At least until she could dry her clothes out enough to put them on again. Prowling through Sean's clothing wasn't what she'd planned or wanted to do, but surely he would understand.

Cynthia headed down the hall in search of his bedroom. The first room she came to turned out to be an office, not a guest room. The way he felt about his family and not visiting them, he probably didn't think he needed a guest room. Instead of a bed there was a solid oak desk facing the window that looked out over the porch. A desk lamp stood on it and a wooden banker's chair was behind it. The chair looked as if it had been lovingly refinished. The man did have talent. He might believe in being thrifty but he liked quality. Sean was a diverse personality.

At the end of the hall was a larger bedroom. Knowing of these old homes' architectural arrangements, she guessed Sean had removed a wall and remodeled the space into more spacious sleeping quarters. Again the furniture consisted of little more than the bare necessities. The floor was made of glossy dark wood she suspected was original to the house. The windows had full-length wooden blinds. They were partially closed. The oak bed was heavy and made the statement that the person who slept in it was all male. A log cabin patterned quilt was spread across it. A bedside table and lamp sat on one side. A tall chest of drawers stood against another wall. Everything about the room screamed Sean.

Cynthia stepped slowly into it. She was entering a private domain but her curiosity kept her going and, after all, she needed something to wear. Peeking past an open door, she found a modern bath but done in a style that stayed true to the age of the house. She loved the man's taste. Of what she'd seen she wouldn't change a thing about the fixtures of the house.

But there was one thing missing. The feeling of belonging. There were no pictures of anyone. It was as if Sean had no past or future. That saddened her. A good man like him should have people in his life who were important to him.

Going to the chest of drawers, she opened the top drawer. There she found his undershirts. They were too thin. Sean would be able to see straight through it if she borrowed one of those and he returned any time soon. In the second she found a dark T-shirt with the name of the hospital across the front. This would do until she had her clothing dried.

Returning to the kitchen, she found a small room off it containing a washer and dryer. There she tossed in her shirt and bra. It shouldn't take them long to dry. Back in the living room, she turned on the TV again. Maybe something good was on that she could watch until Sean returned. Clicking through the channels, she located a favorite show. Feeling cool and not seeing a throw blanket, she went to Sean's room and removed the quilt from his bed. She would replace it before she left. Surely Sean wouldn't be upset with her making herself at home?

Returning to the living room, she curled into the large armchair and wrapped the quilt around her. She inhaled deeply and smiled. Between the chair, cover and shirt it was almost as if she were in Sean's arms. As she watched a late-night talk show, she grew warm. She yawned and her eyes drifted closed.

CHAPTER SEVEN

SEAN RETURNED HOME closer to daylight than dark. When he'd headed for the hospital, he'd anticipated a quick visit but it had turned into emergency surgery that couldn't wait. He'd had a second to think about Cynthia at his house. All he could do now was hope that she wasn't mad. Not that it would make him feel any less a louse, but maybe she had called for a taxi or one of her brothers to come get her.

From the driveway he could see that the TV was still on. Cynthia would have turned it off if she wasn't still here. He quietly let himself into the house, then thought better of it. What if he scared her? He had no need to worry. Cynthia was sound asleep in his chair.

She looked so small and so right in his large chair wrapped in his grandmother's quilt. As if she belonged there. Quietly he put his keys and phone on the table. He wasn't going to allow her to sleep in a chair any longer. He scooped her into his arms, blanket and all.

She blinked then murmured, "You're home."

He held her against his chest and kissed her temple before he headed to his bedroom. "I am."

"Where're we going?" she mumbled in a sweet, sleep-laden voice.

"My bed. Now, hush. Go back to sleep." In his room he laid her on the bed, gently unrolled her from the blanket.

Was that his T-shirt she was wearing? He wouldn't remove her pants, having already stepped over the propriety line by putting her in bed with him without asking her. Pulling the sheet over her, he then spread the quilt on top of that.

Cynthia wrapped her arms around his pillow with a sigh and brought it against her face.

Sean stood there watching her for a minute. How badly he wanted to properly wake her and show her how much he liked having her in his bed. Instead he found himself a clean pair of underwear and a pair of drawstring lounge pants before heading for the bathroom. There he took a cold shower despite having been looking forward to a hot one when he came home.

When he returned, Cynthia was curled up sound asleep in the middle of his bed. He slipped beneath the covers and rolled to his side, gathering her against his chest. *Perfect.* He would worry about her reaction to his forwardness in the morning. Seconds later he had joined her in sleep.

A wiggle of a warm body beside him woke Sean. There was a pink hazy color in the room. It wasn't daylight yet.

His gaze met Cynthia's.

She scooted away from him as if she had just registered where she was. He made no move to stop her. "What am I doing in bed? With you?"

"I put you here. My guests don't sleep in a chair." Maybe if he kept his actions matter of fact she wouldn't get too upset.

She said quietly, "So you bring all your guests to bed after they go to sleep in your chair?"

His gaze didn't leave hers. "No, you're the first."

Cynthia's eyes widened. "Really? I'm the first woman to share this bed?"

He nodded. "Believe it."

She studied him as if trying to decide if he was telling the truth or not. She looked at his bare chest. Lingered. He willed his obvious arousal to ease, but that was wasted effort. That wasn't happening.

Cynthia's attention moved lower. Her voice went a note higher. "You're wearing pants."

"Are you disappointed?" He watched different expressions play across her face at his innuendo. First questioning, contemplating, and then possibility.

"I don't know. Yes, no. Maybe."

"It's simple. I came home far later than I anticipated and you were slumped in the chair. I felt bad and would have felt worse if you'd woken up in pain from sleeping that way. All I did was move you in here. I'd had a long night and needed sleep as well. We're just two friends sharing the same blanket." Someone needed to tell his libido that.

"Oh," she said.

Had she sounded a little disappointed?

Cynthia moved away from him. "It's still not

sunrise. You need your rest. I'll just go finish sleeping on the sofa."

Sean reached across the space between them and caught her hand. How like her to always take the rougher road so that she could make it easier on someone else. "I wish you would stay. There's enough room for us both here."

Her uncertainty was charming.

"Please. I would feel better about going back to sleep." For certain his body would be happier if she was close.

Cynthia covered a yawn with her hand. "Okay."

"Good." Sean settled under the covers again. A second later he felt Cynthia do the same.

He drifted off to sleep with her warmth just inches away. The next time he woke it was to dim light and the splatter of rain on the window. Cynthia was curled against his side as if she had been seeking warmth. Her head lay on his bicep and an arm across his waist. If she knew would she be upset?

He didn't move, savoring the feel of having her near. She was a mass of contradictions. Soft and tender yet strong and demanding. Being around her made life interesting. Had made him start rethinking his. The value she placed on relationships with family almost made him physically nervous.

But right now she was causing a number of other physical issues for him. He wanted her and wanted her badly.

She looked adorable with her hair mussed, her cheeks pink from resting on his pillow, and wearing his T-shirt. The shirt material was pulled tight across her breasts and the outline of her nipple showed. His body twitched. What would she do if he ran a finger across her nipple? Would her eyes open wide in surprise? Or flutter open with wonder? Would she roll away? Did he dare find out which? Could he stop himself?

The tips of Cynthia's fingers brushed his side. His body thrummed with need. His gaze jerked up to find hers. She was watching him. His eyes questioned. Her hand skimmed across his belly and back again, making his skin ripple.

Sean understood when a woman was sending out signals that she wanted him but this forwardness seemed out of character for Cynthia. He had her pegged as the cautious type. Everything about her screamed she was a woman who took being with a man as more than a simple enjoyment of bodies. For her it would involve emotion. Caring. Tomorrow. Could she possibly feel that way about him?

Despite his desires, he had to know before his baser instincts took over. What if she wasn't ready? He'd all but insisted she stay in his bed. Worse, he'd brought her here when she wasn't thinking clearly. Would she see it as him taking advantage of her? He'd never been this indecisive about wanting or having a woman. But if Cynthia said no would he have the strength to roll away from her?

Trying not to base his decisions on the demands of his body, he growled, "Cynthia, if you want to leave this bed untouched then you'd better go now."

There was a pause, then her hand moved again, this time a little further down. "And if I don't want to?"

He glared at her. "Don't tease a man on the edge."

She kissed his chest and murmured, "Ever thought I might be on edge too?"

That was all the invitation he required. He

quickly rolled her on her back. Her head sank into his pillow and the mattress dipped as he came down on her. He supported himself above her and studied her face for a few seconds before his mouth claimed hers.

She opened for him and he found her wet heat waiting to greet him. Her arms wrapped around his neck as she joined him in the twists and turns of a dance of passion. This uninhibited Cynthia he hadn't expected, but she fueled his desire like no other. His lips left hers to tease one corner of her mouth as his hands slipped under her shirt. Her hands kneaded his back as if she were begging for all he could give her. There would be red marks on his skin but he would wear them proudly.

He cupped one of her breasts. Cynthia took his lower lip into her mouth and sucked it. The actions sent a hot flash of desire through him. He was aroused to the point of pain. His heart thumped against his chest wall. If he didn't have her soon he would explode.

When he rolled her nipple between two fingers she flexed her hips, brushing his length. Sean kissed her again as he lifted off her enough to locate the button of her pants. After flipping it open, he deftly moved to the zipper and tugged. Becoming almost frantic in his need to be inside her, he pulled his mouth away. Taking a deep breath, he searched her face.

"This is going too fast. Not fair to you." His breathing was jagged. He had to find control.

"I'm not complaining." She shimmied from side to side until she'd gotten her pants down then cupped his face. "Kiss me. I like it when you kiss me."

He didn't give her time to ask again. He supported himself on one arm, his mouth finding hers. His other hand he placed on her smooth, flat stomach.

"So silky sweet," he murmured.

Cynthia sucked in her stomach, then released it so that it met his palm once more. Her hands gripped his upper arms and squeezed. His hand moved lower until it encountered the lace of her underwear. She hissed. Seconds later, she opened her legs. He cupped her center. She was hot and damp. Ready for him.

His hunger was driven to the breaking point. Sliding his finger under her panties, he explored expertly. Cynthia sucked in a sharp breath; her hips rose and settled, accepting him. Her legs relaxed, allowing him complete access. Small panting sounds filled the air between them as he teased and touched her.

Sean pulled his mouth from hers. He wanted to watch her. Wanted her to know it was him giving her pleasure. Her eyelids were leaden, her mouth slightly open, and her hands running over his chest. He'd never seen anything more erotic in his life. It was intoxicating to see Cynthia so enthralled in the delights he was providing. The tip of his thumb flicked her pleasure spot and her hips lurched upward. He drew his finger out and slipped in again. Cynthia squirmed, then moaned soft and long as she lowered to the bed. Seconds later she opened eyes that held a dreamy look. Her tender smile welcomed him.

He quickly stood, pushed his pants to the floor and kicked them away. Shoving the blanket and sheet to the end of the bed, he pulled her legs around so they hung over the edge of the mattress. Working quickly, he removed her pants from her ankles, letting them fall. When he reached for her panties he found her hands already there. She had them over her hips and he pulled them the rest of the way down her shapely legs. Those he planned to have around his hips soon.

Going to the bath, he took a box out from under the counter and removed a package. Returning to the bed, he watched Cynthia's face as she looked at his naked body. He stepped closer, opening the foil package as he went. When she licked her lips he almost went to his knees. Covering his throbbing length, he made the final step to the bed. She opened her legs so that he could stand between them and admire her sprawled across his bed. Waiting on him. Had there ever been anything more stunning?

Hands on each side of her head, he leaned over her. His lips found hers, tasting and sipping her sweetness. Lowering himself, he nudged against her. Cynthia's hands slid to his hips and tugged him to her. Did she want him as much as he wanted her? In his urgency, his kiss deepened as he entered her.

Sean sucked in a breath and counted to three as he released it. Had he ever been this hot for a woman? This close to bursting?

She wrapped her legs around his hips and squeezed until he filled her completely. Had anything ever been as good as this?

Seconds later he pulled back.

Cynthia made a sound of frustration and he returned to her. She sighed. He repeated the movement a little faster. Picked up the pace. She joined him until they found a rhythm unique to them. As their tempo built Cynthia tensed, lifted higher and gripped his shoulders, her fingers biting in. He made one final thrust, filling her again to the hilt.

A shudder rocked her body. She threw back her head, arched, keening her pleasure before slowly easing to the bed. He searched for their rhythm again. The drum roll built until he found his release and collapsed on top of her. She pulled him into her arms. He'd been welcomed home.

Cynthia knew what it was to have physical relations with a man but had never experienced anything like the magic she'd just shared with Sean. Her heart was full. She regarded her lover's face with wonder, so close and so dear. How had Sean managed to break through her wall to bring her to this point? She smiled. All it had taken was his silver-tongued voice speaking into her ears.

He slowly rolled to lay beside her. Suddenly self-conscious about lying in the light with a naked man, she pulled the sheet across her hips. She was out of her element. Had acted far more a wanton than ever before.

"Don't cover yourself. Didn't I tell you how perfect you are? Amazing?"

She wasn't used to men praising her body. Her ex certainly hadn't fawned over her. To have Sean say those words warmed her, made her feel cherished. When was the last time she'd felt special? This was what it was like to have a man admire her. She planned to bask in it.

"Cyn. That suits you." His hand ran up her bare thigh. "You sure make me think about sinning."

Cynthia liked hearing her nickname from his lips. Her family members were the only ones who called her that. Sean had moved into her inner circle so easily and quickly. Now she didn't want him to ever leave.

"That's the nicest compliment I've ever had." She moved to face him, caressing him with her eyes. Sean had a beautiful body. All vast plains with hollows and slopes. He seemed so at ease with himself. Had she been built like him, she might be self-confident as well. Unable to resist, she reached across his chest and ran her fingertips over his ribs and circled a blue spot on his side.

She reversed her hand. "I'm sorry you got all bruised up in the paintball fight."

"I'm not. It was fun."

Cynthia continued to learn the valleys and plains of his chest, then the dips and highs of his ribs.

"I would be careful about that. I might make you pay for tickling me." His breath brushed her ear. She shivered. He chuckled.

"I bet you would." Insecurity washed through her. Had she been too forward? Too loud? Was he disappointed?

"Hey." He tugged gently at a lock of her hair. "Is something wrong?"

Did her feelings show so clearly or was Sean that good at reading her? "I'm just not sure why you're interested in me when you could have anyone."

In a near angry tone he announced, "You're going to make me mad with talk like that. Are you making me a cliché again? I can't imagine why a woman who's capable in so many diverse areas, and beautiful to boot, could possibly wonder why me or any other man wouldn't want her. Fear not, you satisfy me both in and out of bed."

A feeling she didn't want to put a name to filled her heart.

"The problem now is mine. How will I ever get enough of you?" Sean asked, as if he needed her to take pity on him.

Cynthia's heart was near to bursting. "Doctor, I like your bedside manner. You sure know the right thing to say."

Sean smiled. Cynthia made him feel as if he were the most special man in the world. He should have known he would be tempting fate to bring her to his bed. There was no way he wouldn't want more of her. He'd never felt for anyone the way he cared about her. Even now his mind and body wanted more. What was going on with him? He felt edgy, as if something were happening that was out of his control. He needed to figure this out. Rein in his emotions.

"Hey, what time is it?" Cynthia exclaimed.

Sean looked over his shoulder at the alarm clock on the bedside table. "Nine fifty-two."

Cynthia leaped up and grabbed her clothes. "I've got to go. The boys are going to be wondering where I am. I've never been gone this long without checking in."

He sat up and caught her around the wrist as she turned to walk away. "You do know they're not boys any more? I'd bet they know all about the birds and the bees."

Her cheeks went red. It was refreshing to find a woman who could still be self-conscious about sex. "I know, but that doesn't mean I have to make a show of not being there. Me sleeping over with a man for any reason is highly unusual."

Sean let go of her and stood. Taking her hand, he brought her up close and gazed into her eyes. "What you're saying is that I'm special?"

Cynthia's gaze didn't waver. "Very. You've been that from the moment I first heard your voice."

He brought his mouth close to her ear, lips skimming it. “So you like it when I whisper sweet nothings in your ear?”

“Yes.” She lightly pushed at his chest. “Now you’re trying to distract me. I’ve got to go.”

“I’ll let you go for now but only if you’ll tell me more about how much you like my voice later.”

She huffed. “Men and their egos. I promise. Do you mind if I get a quick shower?”

“Not at all. Make yourself at home.” In the short time she’d been in his house she’d already managed to make her mark on his very personal spaces. His chair, his bed and now she wanted to leave him memories of her in his bath.

While he picked up his clothing she headed to the bath. Seconds later he joined her.

“Is something wrong?” she asked, eyes wide when he entered.

“Nope. I just thought I’d join you. I need to drive you home, remember? Also, I have patients to see in the office this afternoon.”

“I can wait until you get through in here.” She reached for her clothes.

Sean lightly caught hold of her wrist. "I thought we could share the shower."

She looked anywhere but at him. "I don't know."

He reached in and turned the water on. "I'll even let you have the spot under the shower-head."

She looked at his large tile shower and then back at him. "I guess we could do that."

And much more if he had his way. He fingered the hem of his T-shirt she still wore. It fell to the top of her thigh. "Don't get me wrong and I don't care that you're wearing it but would you mind telling me why you have on my favorite T-shirt?"

Cynthia shifted and the shirt pulled against her breasts. His body twitched in awareness. He'd not taken the time he should have to appreciate the gifts hidden beneath the tee.

She looked down as if she'd forgotten what she was wearing. "I got my shirt and bra wet. I needed something to wear while drying them. I borrowed your shirt and fell asleep before my clothes were finished drying."

"It looks far better on you than it does on me."

He studied the shape of her breasts and the outline of her nipples pushed against the material. Unable to resist, he touched one.

Cynthia drew in a breath and went still. Her eyes widened. That was enough to encourage him. He cupped her breast, tested its weight. “Perfect.”

His hands found her hips. “As fetching as you look in my shirt, I know I would enjoy what’s beneath much more.”

Sean ran his hands along her curves until he had gathered the shirt around her hands raised above her head. Her beautiful full breasts were completely exposed to him. Unable to stand it any longer, he took a nipple into his mouth. Cynthia inhaled with a hiss. His tongue circled her nipple and he tugged gently with his teeth before releasing it.

He removed the shirt to find her staring at him with desire-glazed eyes. He grinned, already responding to having her naked. She shivered. “Come on. The water should be warm. I know you’re in a hurry to go.”

“Not that big of one,” she murmured.

He chuckled as he followed her in under the

water. No woman had been as responsive or open to his lovemaking as Cynthia. She seemed to bask in wonder and pleasure at his every touch.

She was under the water with her face up when he closed the glass door behind himself. Sean stepped up behind her. Placing his hands on her small waist, he pressed against her backside. He wanted her to know what she did to him. She shifted back to press herself against him. Once again she amazed him. Clearly she didn't mind letting him know she wanted him. There was nothing timid about her lovemaking. It was open and full on.

Was that what this was? Sex had always been enjoyable but with Cynthia it went to a high level. But love? That he'd never been a part of before. It scared him. He liked what he and Cynthia shared but was it more than two people who really connected?

Sean kissed the top of her shoulder. She shuddered. His hands slid up her torso to cup both of her breasts. She leaned back against his chest giving him full access. Her hands came around to grip his thighs. He gently pulled and teased her breasts as he placed little kisses along her neck and jaw. "I have to taste you."

He slowly turned her to face him. She looked at him as if he were the most amazing man in the world. Somehow he was going to see to it that she always believed that. Bending, he took a wet, swollen nipple into his mouth. She whimpered so sweetly he was afraid he might not be able to last. Gaining control, he moved to the other nipple, giving it the same attention.

With one hand, she hung onto his shoulder while the other slipped over his thigh up to his hip. There she hesitated before she took him in her hand. His blood boiled and his body throb unbearably. He'd never been set on fire so soon after having a woman. It was usually once and done and he was on his way home.

He had to step away or lose his mind. She deserved her pleasure as well. If she continued to move her hand he'd detonate. As he stepped back, her hand slowly slipped over him, which was worse than her earlier administrations.

Cynthia raised her worried eyes to meet his. "Did I do something wrong?"

"No. If anything it was too right. I want to give

you pleasure this time. Nothing rushed. If you kept that up it would end up being all about me. I want this time to be about you." He dropped to a knee. Reaching around her, he grabbed her supple behind and pulled her to him. Kissing her stomach as the water ran over them. "Put a leg over my shoulder."

Her eyes widened. "I don't—"

"Please. For me."

She delayed another moment before complying. His arm went around her waist as her hand went to his shoulder. The other fingered his hair.

Sean dipped his tongue in, finding her hot center. A moan of pure animal pleasure rolled out of Cynthia. Lust rocked like thunder through him. She pressed forward. He gave her what she desired. Her grip on his shoulder tightened. She went up on her toes. He stroked his tongue against her again. She tensed and her hand left his shoulder to brace against the wall while the one on his head brought his mouth more intimately against her. She stiffened, then shuddered before becoming pliant. Seconds later he hurried to support her. Her forehead rested against his chest, as she breathed deeply.

They stood that way until Sean could stand it no longer. He opened the shower door and led her out.

"What about you?" she mumbled.

"Don't worry. We're going to see about me." His hands came to her waist and lifted her to the bathroom counter. "Scoot to the edge." She did as she was bid. He stepped between her knees and in one swift, smooth move he entered her. Cynthia cupped his face and kissed him as he sank deep. He was so hard for her that he feared the first contact would be all he could stand. He managed a couple of plunges before a white-hot explosion gripped him.

His forehead came to rest on Cynthia's shoulder.

"How do you expect me to walk after that?" she asked as her fingers played with the hair at the nape of his neck.

Sean looked at her with what he was sure was a foolish grin on his lips. "I was going to ask you the same thing."

"That was amazing, Doctor."

He wanted to let out a caveman roar.

A quarter of an hour later, they were finishing dressing when Cynthia said, “I forgot to ask how your patient is doing. Obviously there were more problems than you anticipated.”

“She’ll be fine but she’ll have a long recovery period. It was an ugly accident.”

“I’m glad to hear you could help her. You have a real gift.” She grinned. “For more than one thing.”

She had one as well. Making him feel like the most special person on the planet. That was something he had missed in his life. Would he ever be able to let her go?

CHAPTER EIGHT

CYNTHIA WAS A little worried about arriving home to find Mark waiting. She wasn't prepared for his interrogation right now. As Sean pulled into the drive she was relieved her brother's car was gone. Thank goodness he had to work. She wasn't in the habit of answering to her brothers; usually it was her asking the questions.

Sean reached across the seat and took her hand. She still tingled at his touch, which was amazing since their morning had been so personal. He affected her like no one else. She wanted to throw her hands up in the air and spin around. It was as if she were young again and had dropped all the responsibilities and worries she carried when she was with him. She liked herself. Believed anything was possible.

Sean's smile was sad. "I'd really like to see you tonight but I've got to work on the grant."

She shifted in the seat to face him. "Is it something I can help with?"

"I can always use your help."

"Why don't I fix dinner and you come here? We'll tackle it together." She didn't want to miss a minute of time she could spend with him.

"So I don't feel guilty about making you work every night, why don't you let me get takeout?" he asked, perking up.

"Darn, I forgot. I promised a friend I'd help at the community center tonight. We are feeding the disabled veterans and playing bingo." She never forgot things like that. What was happening to her? Sean was taking over her life. And she liked it.

"Then we'll try for tomorrow night." There was a hopeful note in his voice.

"I'm sorry but Rick has a makeup game." She hated letting Sean down. Hated more not getting to see him. "You could always come."

"I may need to work on the grant. Let me see how much I get done tonight and I'll let you know."

"I should be helping you." Her guilt level was rising.

"You've already done a lot. You can't be everywhere for everybody."

But she wanted to be there for him.

His hand came to rest around her neck, bringing her close. "You know I'd like to have you to myself again."

Warmth radiated out from her heart. She smiled. "I wouldn't mind that at all."

His slow kiss made her toes curl. "How about we try for day after tomorrow? Just us."

"Sounds perfect to me." She was already looking forward to it. "See you then." Minutes later she stood on the porch watching until he drove out of sight. The hours wouldn't pass fast enough until they were together again. She entered the house as if walking on a cloud.

The rest of the day went by while she completed her transcription jobs. There were none from Sean, but she now had the real thing instead of just a voice in her ears. Actual kisses, touches, looks and his body over hers as his fingers worked magic. There was also the laughing. Sean with his quick wit, smiles, and patience. The flesh-and-blood Sean who went with that beautiful voice was so much better than the one she'd imagined.

Would the clock change time soon enough? She was trying to concentrate on work, but her thoughts kept coming back to her fear that her hopes had risen too high about their relationship. Or if they could make one work. She still knew so precious little of what Sean wanted out of life outside of financial security. Was their fledging affection strong enough to last? Did he want it to? Did she?

Just before she was going to stop work for the day she checked her emails. With a quiver of excitement in her core she saw there was one from Sean.

Hey Cyn,

I just wanted to say I've been thinking about you.

You are amazing.

Looking forward to seeing you again soon.

Sean

If she wasn't crazy about him before, she was now. Cynthia reread the note until she had to force herself to get to work.

Finally it was time to get ready to go to the

center. At least she would be busy and not have as much time to think about Sean. No grown woman should act as moonstruck over a man, but she couldn't help it. She couldn't get enough of Sean or keep her anticipation at bay.

Humming a tune, she took an unhurried shower. Memories of their time earlier that morning had her hotter than the water temperature. Every day should start off as wonderful.

She had never considered herself a very liberated person in the bedroom, but with Sean her inhibitions faded away. After a long time of holding back, she'd let go and been herself. Not the woman responsible for her brothers, the house, a job and all the minute details of life. Instead she was Sean Donavon's lover. Being unrestrained was freeing. Liberating. Fun.

An hour later, dressed in a simple light blue blouse and jeans, Cynthia entered the one-story cement block building. As she made her way across the tile floor toward the kitchen, she spoke and joked with several of the men and women already seated at tables. Though her exchanges were upbeat some of the enjoyment had been taken out of the evening. She missed Sean.

Reaching the kitchen, she checked in with her friend, Rose, who was in charge for the night. "What do you want me to do?"

"I'd like you to run the bingo game. The veterans seem to appreciate the special flair you add when you call the numbers."

Cynthia hmphed and picked up the box containing the bingo cards. "I'm sure my occasional use of *uno*, *dos*, or *eins*, *zwei* is very entertaining."

"Maybe not to you, but to them it seems to be," Rose retorted before turning back to the food she was placing in large serving pans.

Forty-five minutes later the meal had been served and Cynthia was standing in front of the room calling out numbers. She was preparing to announce another one when she looked up to see Sean's smiling face. Her heart skipped. Unable to do little more than stare at him when she really wanted to fling herself into his arms, she managed to get the next number out.

He grinned as he took a seat next to an old, grizzled-looking veteran named Mr. Vick sitting at the back table. One of the veterans had to prompt her to call another number because she couldn't get over Sean being there. He looked incredible dressed in his knit shirt and navy trousers, appearing every bit the well-to-do urban male. It should be against the law to look as fabulous as he did. Was he as glad to see her as she was to see him?

Calling numbers as quickly as she could to end the game, she declared a break before the next game and hurried to where Sean sat. He stood as she approached, a hand already out waiting on hers to slip into it. His fingers curled tightly around hers. Breathlessly she demanded, "What're you doing here? You're supposed to be working."

He beamed down at her. "I was. Really hard. But I thought a little bingo might help me unwind."

She gave him a narrow-eyed look. "You came all this way for bingo?"

"That—" he gave her a quick kiss "—and that." He said softly, "I missed you."

"Hey, buddy, are you hitting on Cynthia?" Mr. Vick asked with a wheeze and a cough.

She and Sean looked at him. "Sean, I'd like you to meet Mr. Vick."

To his credit Sean offered his hand. "It's nice to meet you."

Mr. Vick nodded and took it.

"I have to go back to the game. Can you stay until I'm done?" She looked at Sean. "You are welcome to play."

"That's okay. I'll just sit here and watch," Sean said when she pointed to an unused card on the table.

"Come on, don't be a stick in the mud. You might just have some fun," she quipped with a grin.

"I'm no stick in the mud!" He took the card offered, but looked at it as if he had no idea what to do with it.

"Have you ever played bingo before?" She managed not to laugh.

"Well, no," he said sheepishly.

Mr. Vick pushed some markers his way and winked. "I'll show him." Again, there was a wheezing with every word, then a short coughing fit.

She grinned at Sean. "Have fun."

For the next hour she called numbers. Sean even won a game. He whooped and put a hand in the air, pumping it in a sign of victory. He smiled broadly as he came to the front to receive his prize. There was friendly ribbing among the crowd over the possibility of her cheating so he could win. A few games later Rose called an end to the play.

As Cynthia boxed up the supplies Sean approached her. "So I'm guessing by your reaction to winning you're now a fan of bingo. Another first for you too."

"I have to admit I had a good time." There was a twinkle in his eye.

"That's what's important." She smiled at him.

His face turned serious. "Do you think Mr. Vick trusts you enough that he'd let me examine him if you asked?"

"I guess so. Is something wrong?" She glanced at the older man starting for the door.

"I think I know what might be causing that wheeze he has. It could be serious if it isn't taken care of."

Cynthia didn't hesitate before calling, "Mr. Vick." He turned to face them. "Wait up a minute, would you?" She and Sean walked toward him. "Mr. Vick, I was wondering if you would tell us about when your wheeze started? Sean here is a doctor and he's curious."

The man looked stricken and raised his hand to his throat.

Cynthia gave him a reassuring touch on the arm. "It's okay. Nothing'll happen you don't agree to."

"Mr. Vick, did you hurt your throat some time ago?" Sean asked, studying the man closely.

The grizzled man nodded.

"I'm a doctor who takes care of those types of things. I think you might have the beginnings of a real problem. I'd like to examine your throat."

Mr. Vick started shaking his head. "Don't like doctors."

"I can understand that but I promise I'll just touch your throat and look down it. Nothing more."

"I'll be right here with you. I promise Sean will be easy on you," Cynthia added confidently. She knew his tenderness first hand.

The man looked from her to Sean and back again, then nodded.

"Cynthia, would you see if you can find me

a flashlight?" Sean had turned into a medical professional on a mission.

"There should be one in the kitchen. I'll be right back." She hurried off and returned minutes later.

Sean had Mr. Vick sitting in a chair and was slowly moving his fingers along his throat.

"Here you go." Cynthia handed him the flashlight.

"Mr. Vick, please open your mouth as wide as you can." Sean shined the light into the man's mouth. Seconds later he straightened and turned off the light. "Mr. Vick, you have a tracheal stenosis. I'm afraid it can be serious. Have you had pneumonia more than once?"

A wheezy "Yes" came from the man.

"You'll have it again. It will get worse each time you have it. You'll start having to stay in the hospital. I could help you if you would let me." Sean waited as if the man saying yes was extremely important to him.

Mr. Vick took some time before he asked, "How?"

"It's a pretty simple procedure done with a

laser. You'll need to stay one night in the hospital but that's about it."

Mr. Vick stood. "Let me think about it."

"If money is the problem, don't worry about it."

Cynthia's heart swelled. Sean might not believe in spending money on frivolous things but he would take care of a veteran without batting an eye.

Sean pulled his wallet out, found a card and handed it to him. "This has my office number on it. Call and make an appointment when you get ready. Tell them I told you to call."

"Okay." The ever-present wheeze was there.

"But don't wait too long," Sean added as Mr. Vick walked away.

"Do you think he'll call?" Cynthia asked.

"I hope so. Sooner rather than later." Sean turned to her. "Are you ready to go?"

"Yeah, just as soon as I put the bingo stuff up in the cabinet." She started toward the box sitting on the table up front.

Minutes later they were on their way out of the door into the dimly lit parking lot. Cynthia walked toward her car and Sean followed beside her. She didn't want their time together to end but she was unsure what she should do next. What was happening between them was too new. When they arrived at her car she faced him. "It was sure a nice surprise to see you tonight. Real nice."

Sean stepped closer, forcing her back against the door. "Nice enough that I can get a thank-you kiss?"

Her arms went around his neck and she went up on her toes to give it to him. Seconds later Sean pulled her tightly against him as he took charge of the kiss. All she'd experienced that morning had been real.

"I can't seem to get enough of you," he whispered with wonder in his voice.

She gazed at his face. "I missed you too. Thanks for the email."

"You're welcome." His lips found hers again.

When a couple of veterans walked by them, she and Sean broke apart.

"Hey, are you hungry?" Sean asked. There was a desperate note in his voice. As if he wanted to hang onto her longer.

"A little," she admitted.

"How about going for dessert?" He took her hand and pulled her toward his car parked a couple of spots away.

She giggled. "Okay."

Sean found a diner not far away. He wasn't going to let Cynthia go for the night until he had to. He led her to a back corner booth. When she stopped in the middle of the seat he said, "Scoot over," and sat next to her.

Cynthia was obviously pleased with his decision. She smiled brightly. There was a rightness about being next to her that had him thinking of more than just tonight.

When the waitress came to take their order they both asked for a slice of pecan pie. She ordered hot tea and he a coffee.

Taking her hand under the table, he brought it to his thigh and held it there. He wished he could find some way to have her to himself for just a little while. They both had busy lives but hers seemed as if it were wrapped up in doing for everyone but herself. He liked that she cared, had such a big heart, but she needed to move forwards in life. He knew from pleasurable experience that all of the business covered up an uninhibited Cynthia who was amazing.

She leaned her head against his shoulder and squeezed his bicep. "It's so nice to see you."

He smiled. "I couldn't stay away."

Cynthia turned to him. "What about your grant? How much did you get done on it?"

His look held hers. "Surprisingly a whole lot. Maybe it was because I was so anxious to see you and wouldn't let myself leave until I reached my goal for the night."

"So I was the prize?"

"You were." He kissed her.

The waitress brought their order. Just as Cynthia was about to take her first bite of pie she asked in a worried tone, "What time is it?"

Sean checked his watch. "Nine fifteen."

"Oh, no, I'm late." She started burrowing through her pocketbook.

Sean put down his coffee cup, preparing to leave. "For what?"

"To check in with my brothers. We do it every night at nine if one of us is out." She tapped a number on her phone.

Her obsession with her brothers was a little

over the top. He understood concern or caring to a point but it was as if she couldn't accept that her brothers were grown men. If her relationship with him went further, could she let go of them enough to share her life with him?

As she spoke to Mark then Rick Sean finished his pie and coffee.

Done, she smiled at him and pulled her pie plate to her.

"Help out veterans and check on your brothers. You're always taking care of someone. Who takes care of you?"

She shrugged. "I guess I do. I just do what my mother did. What my father encouraged us to do. See about each other."

"That must be hard doing everything by yourself. I don't see how that leaves much time for that fun you keep talking about."

She looked at him over the rim of her tea cup. "Sometimes that is hard to find. But I try."

Sean put his arm across the back of the seat. Her shoulder brushed the tips of his fingers and that was all it took for his body to react. How long could he endure sitting so close without kissing her again?

"So tell me what I can do to help with the work on the grant." Cynthia pushed her half-eaten pie away.

"See, there you go wanting to help me."

Cynthia gave him a sideways glance. "You do still need it, don't you?"

"Yeah. I made a list of things I need to finish. There are a couple on there that I could use your help with."

"Email me the list and I'll get right on them first thing in the morning." Cynthia seemed truly excited to assist him. More than that she was being supportive of him. Something that he'd known little of when he was a kid. "It's nice to be needed."

"You're needed all right." He scooted out of the booth, took her hand, pulling her up to stand beside him. "I think I should take you somewhere private to thank you properly." He paid the bill and escorted her to the car.

Minutes later he parked next to her vehicle in the empty lot of the community center.

He took her in his arms and nuzzled her neck. Slowly his lips traveled across her cheek until his mouth found hers. Her hand came up to rest on his neck. He loved the feel of her fingers in his hair. The kiss was deep, hot and carnal. He wanted her to the point of pain.

Cynthia yelped when her elbow hit the gear shift. He pulled back, uttering a descriptive word under his breath. Giving her a wry grin, he said, "I'm far too old and too big to make out in a car."

She giggled. "But I was enjoying it."

"I was too. Too much."

"I need to go anyway. My brothers will be wondering where I am."

Would they really? He would guess not. They seemed to have moved on with their lives while Cynthia continued to live as if her parents were alive. It had to have been tough to virtually become a parent of two teenagers when she was barely out of her teens herself but it was time to let go. Time for her to live some. "What would it take for me to have you all to myself?"

"You will day after tomorrow." She moved back to the passenger seat.

"That's not enough." He sounded as if he were begging, as he had when he'd wanted his parents' attention. "But I guess I'll settle for what I can get."

She kissed him behind his ear. "I'll..." then she kissed his temple "...make..." then the arch of his brow "...it..." the end of his nose "... worth..." the corner of his mouth "...your..." she nipped at his bottom lip "...while." The tip of her tongue traced the line of his mouth. "Promise."

His straining, painful arousal made a cold shower a sure thing tonight.

"You're a tease. I'm going to hold you to that. I expect you to keep that promise."

Cynthia kissed him. "Count on it. I'd better go." She pulled her pocketbook strap over her shoulder and stepped out of the car.

Sean joined her. She reached her arms around his waist, pulled him to her and kissed him. Sean brought her against him and lifted her off her feet. Long, delightful minutes later he reluctantly let her slowly slide down him. "Good night, Cynthia."

That night in Cynthia's bed had been lonely and cold, and incredibly long without Sean. There was an email waiting on her the next morning.

Cyn,
Quick note: crazy day ahead.

I had planned to make Rick's game but have to speak to a patient about an issue involving the grant app. Tonight is the only time he can do it.

Sorry.

I'll be home by six thirty tomorrow. See you then.

Miss you.

Sean

P.S. List attached

Cynthia couldn't deny she was disappointed. She had held out hope he would surprise her as he had the night before and make the game. She so wanted to see him. But he was doing something important.

She emailed back.

Hey,

Hope your day smooths out. I miss you too. Already looking forward to tomorrow. I'll bring dinner!

Cyn

That night Rick's basketball game didn't hold much interest for her. Every minute that ticked by on the clock was a minute she was closer to seeing Sean again. The hours dragged by the next day despite her efforts to keep busy. Finally, she was almost to Sean's house. The traffic wasn't heavy so she made good time. Excitement bubbled in her. The last two days had been the longest she'd lived through since her parents had died.

She had it bad for Sean Donavon and she didn't see any way back. The question was did Sean feel the same way? Or was he having that fun she'd encouraged him to have at her expense?

The minute she pulled into his driveway the front door opened and Sean stepped out. A large smile was on his face. He was obviously glad to see her. Still wearing his usual workday attire, he had pulled his shirttail out of his pants. The slightly rumpled look on him was appealing. He appeared relaxed, as if he was a little more at ease with life. Did he realize this?

It was nice to have someone excited to see her. It had been a long time since something in her life had revolved around her. So much of her time had been about her brothers or them as a family. Rarely had it been about her. Had she kept it that way for them or for her?

Sean met her as she stepped out of the car.

"Hey there," she breathed.

He grabbed her and lifted her tightly against him as if he'd found a precious belonging that had gone missing. Her arms went around his neck. His mouth found hers. The kiss made it clear on many levels he was glad to see her. When he pulled back he said, staring into her eyes, "I've missed you."

Cynthia kept her arms wrapped around his neck and beamed at him. "I wish you'd taken the time to show me."

"Funny girl. That's what I like about you—you always have jokes." He let her go to stand on her feet.

She turned serious. "I like a lot of things about you too."

"You keep looking at me like that and the neighbors are going to see exactly how well I like you."

Cynthia glanced around to see if anyone was watching. "Didn't you just show them that?"

His voice went into a low growl. "The real show would be much grander."

She murmured, "We might need to move that

one inside. Dinner's in the bag on the backseat. Would you get it?"

"Sure. But food isn't what I'm thinking about right now." Sean winked at her and took the sack out of the car.

They walked toward the front door.

"So what do you have in mind for tonight? Working on your grant? Watching another Western?" she teased.

Sean opened the door, stood back allowing her to enter ahead of him.

Cynthia laid her purse on the table next to his keys. There was something intimate about their belongings sharing the same space. "Let me have that bag. The coleslaw needs to go in the refrigerator unless you're ready to eat now."

"I'll see to it." He walked to the kitchen with more purpose than required for food care.

"So how did the meeting go last night?" Cynthia asked as she joined him.

"Very well. I marked one thing off the list." He sat the bag on the counter and inspected its contents.

"Did you have a chance to do any more on

it?" Cynthia watched him. She'd missed him last night with every fiber of her being.

He located the plastic bowl, pulled it out and opened the refrigerator door. "Not much."

"Then you'll be pleased to know that I accomplished three."

Sean looked at her and smiled. "Whatever did I do without you?"

She hoped he never had to find out. "When is it due?"

"Next Monday." Coleslaw on the shelf, he pushed the refrigerator door shut with more force than necessary. He stalked toward her. Taking her hand, he tugged her through the living room and down the hall. "I'm not really interested in talking about that. I have other things on my mind I'd rather be doing."

"Such as?" she asked sweetly as she made a half-effort to drag her feet.

He stopped and she just managed not to stumble. Sean had a determined glint in his eye. "Like examining you without clothes."

Cynthia looked at him as innocently as she could manage. "So, what you're saying is that you're only interested in my body."

He growled low in his throat. “You know good and well I have the highest esteem for your mind but right now I’d like to enjoy your body.”

Cynthia stopped resisting and they entered his room. “Don’t you think we should sit down and talk some?” she said amiably. “After all, we haven’t seen each other in a couple of days.” She was unable to keep the grin from her face as he had her sit on the bed.

“You’re welcome to talk all you want while I’m doing this.” He nuzzled behind her ear.

Cynthia shivered and a soft *mmm* escaped her. She tilted her head, giving him better access to her neck.

Sean lifted his head and looked at her with a twinkle in his eye. “What? No chatter? I thought you were going to talk.”

“You keep that up and we won’t need any words.” She lay back on the bed, pulling him to her. Her hands went under his shirt tail and found warm skin.

His lips moved close to hers. “I think our bodies are long overdue for a conversation.”

Cynthia’s hips flexed against him. “Talk all you want.”

An hour later they were sitting at his kitchen table, eating. Sean wore only a pair of worn jeans. Cynthia could hardly concentrate on her meal for watching the ripple of muscles across his chest. She'd pulled on one of his T-shirts that she'd rejected as too thin the other night.

"You're staring at me," he said between bites of coleslaw.

"I would think you would be used to it." Cynthia's gaze didn't waver.

"Why's that?"

"Because you're so good-looking." She couldn't believe he didn't know it.

"Who says that?" Doubt filled his voice.

"Me. You're almost breathtaking."

He looked up and grinned at her. "Breathtaking, eh?"

"Now I've messed up. That's going straight to your head. I'll hear about that forever."

He leaned in close. His eyes remained fixed on hers. "Would you like to hear about it forever?"

Cynthia's heart skipped a beat then righted itself. What was he really asking? Was he talking about forever between them? How should she answer that? "I could stand that."

"Just stand?" His look didn't waver.

"I would like that," she said with all the conviction she felt.

"Me too." Sean leaned over and kissed her. "We are good together."

Had he just said he loved her in an around about way? It didn't matter. He cared about her. No one talked about forever with someone they didn't truly care about.

They ate for a few more minutes before Sean said, "I hate to do this to you but I've got to work on the grant application some tonight. Do you mind?"

"Not at all. Is there something I can do?" She took a drink of iced tea.

He pushed back in his chair. "I was hoping you'd ask. I have one small project."

"Do I need my laptop for it? I didn't bring it." She wouldn't be much help after all.

"You will, but you can use mine."

She stood. "I'm going to put my pants on. I feel a little underdressed to be working."

"It's probably just as well, because if you sashay around here with that cute behind showing I'm not going to be able to concentrate."

She looked down at him. "So you're saying that I disturb you?"

"Yeah, a lot." His voice turned stern. "Now, go and get back here and help me." He grinned and gave her a light pop on the behind.

"Ouf," she said, and giggled.

Sean had never enjoyed being around a woman as much as he did Cynthia. Their relationship was playful. Fun. He liked having fun. More than one of his woman friends had called him uptight.

His parents had accused him of being an old man in a young man's body. Those had been times when he'd been disgusted with them over being excited about a new product or plan. After a while he'd stopped even complaining. For him most of the enthusiasm had been taken out of life except where his work was concerned. With Cynthia, he laughed. Her quick wit made him think. Life had become pleasurable, something he looked forward to. She gave him something he hadn't realized was missing in his life. Laughter. As Cynthia would call it, fun.

They had talked around the subject of forever earlier. She seemed as if she wanted the same things as him but he'd held back on telling her what he felt. But did he really know? Their relationship was so fresh yet he knew it was something special. For a little while longer he would settle for just enjoying having her in his life.

They worked for a few hours and he was pleased with what they had accomplished.

"I should be done tomorrow. I'll review it and it'll be ready to go before next Monday." He was optimistic that he would receive the grant.

"I'm glad." She stood and put her arms around his neck, giving him a hug from behind. "I'm proud of you."

His heart swelled. When was the last time someone had said that to him? Cynthia knew how to make a person feel special.

Sean brought her around him to sit on his lap. "Thanks for your help."

Her arm lay along his shoulders and her fingers caressed the shell of his ear. "All part of a transcriptionist's service."

"I think you've gone above the call of duty." He kissed her temple.

"Maybe, but I'm still glad I could help. As much as I hate it I've got to go. It's getting late." She slipped off his legs.

"Go? Can't you stay the night? I hate for you to have to drive home so late." He took her hand and pulled her back toward him.

"Sean, you know I can't. I have to think about the example I'm setting for the boys."

For once Sean would like her to think of them before her brothers. Would Cynthia ever put her wants ahead of others'? Let her brothers grow up in her mind? He made a point of using an even tone and not sounding antagonistic. "So the idea is we'll just catch each other here and there?"

She slumped and gave him a sad look. "I guess we'll just have to play it day by day. I can't come over on the nights Rick has games. You're always welcome to go with me to those."

Sean stood and put his hands on her shoulders. "I have to be honest. I want more but I'll take what I can get. For now." He kissed her.

"I'm sorry it has to be this way for now. I need

to get my clothes and shoes." Cynthia headed for the bedroom.

Sean's frustration was growing with her constant need to treat her brothers as if they were children. They were adults just as she was and it was time for her to treat them as such. Sean cleaned up what they had been working on and met her in the living room. "I'll walk you out." He took her hand.

At the car, he brought her close and kissed her with all the passion he felt. She returned it. With every fiber in his being screaming *no*, he let her go.

CHAPTER NINE

SEAN MANAGED TO make one of Rick's basketball games that week. He had to admit he had a good time but he still wished he could spend more time alone with Cynthia, instead of competing with everything else in her life.

Still, the last few days had been wonderful. The nicest he could remember. He'd even enjoyed the family aspect of it. There was a feeling of belonging that he'd not known in a long time. Even acceptance. Her family was one he could be proud of. He puffed with pride when Rick was named most valuable player at the end of the game.

Cynthia did spend Sunday in his bed. After making long, lazy love they were wrapped in each other's arms when she asked, "So the grant application is ready to go?"

"First thing in the morning. Now all I have to do is wait."

"That'll probably be the worst part." She frowned, then brightened. "We should celebrate."

The idea startled him. He never thought to do that. "Like how?"

"You know. Have some fun."

There was that word again. "Don't we need to save that until we know if I get it?" Sean asked as he ran a finger along her arm.

"No, we should do something special." She sat up and looked at him while pulling the sheet up to cover her gorgeous breasts.

"What we were doing just now was fun." He snatched the sheet away.

"Stop." She grabbed at the material. "I want you to concentrate on what I'm saying."

He did have a hard time thinking straight when she was naked.

She looked at him earnestly. "Making love is enjoyable but you need to let loose some, Dr. Donavon. Go somewhere, do something. Have *fun*."

Could this be a chance to get her to himself for a little while? No interruptions. No having her running home. Fun wasn't something he was well versed in but he knew how he'd like to celebrate. By having Cynthia all to himself. "Maybe that's not such a bad idea."

She perked up. Excitement filled her voice. "What would we do?"

"Something like you and me going away for a few days. I have a buddy who has been trying to get me to use his cabin on a lake north of here. We can celebrate there. He said something about it being available next weekend. How does that sound?"

Cynthia withered, seemed unsure. After a few seconds, she rallied to say in a cheery voice, "Okay, that sounds nice. I'd like that. Rick's season is over this Tuesday night so I'm free." She grinned. "And I like going to a lake even in the early spring."

"Then I'll set it up."

Monday afternoon there was an email in Cynthia's box:

Cyn,
I got our trip to the lake all set up for this weekend. Let's plan to leave about three.
Looking forward to having you to myself.
Sean

She anticipated the coming weekend like a child waiting to open a long-expected gift. An entire weekend with Sean sounded like pure heaven. The last week, despite the juggling of their schedules, had been amazing. She'd never been happier or felt more complete.

As she daydreamed the phone rang. She picked up her phone hoping it might be Sean.

"Cyn." It was Mark.

"Hey, what's going on?"

"My car has died." He sounded disgusted.

"Where're you?" She was already thinking about where they were going to get the money to pay for the repairs.

"I made it to work but it was smoking when I got here. I don't know if it can be fixed. I'm going to have the guy here give it a look but it doesn't look good."

"All right." This was all they needed.

"I'm going to need to borrow your car to get to work the rest of this week," Mark said.

"I know. I'll be there to pick you up after work." And she wouldn't be going to Sean's to-night.

She emailed him:

Hey Sean,
You don't know how much I hate it, but I'm not going to make it tonight. Mark has had car trouble and needs me to pick him up.

I won't make the rest of the week either, as he'll need my car to get to work. You're welcome here anytime.

I can't wait until this weekend.

Sorry…
Cyn

Sean wasn't going to like that email at all. More than once she'd noticed his lips thinning into a tight line before he'd realized she was watching him as she'd mentioned something she needed to do for her brothers. But with the weekend coming up she planned to focus all her attention on him. With his family background, he must have felt as if he was secondary to anything her brothers were doing. She never meant for him to feel that way but it must seem so to him.

Cynthia had already told Mark and Rick she'd be gone over the weekend and could be reached by phone. They'd had a few questions and grinned at her knowingly but otherwise hadn't been interested. Maybe they didn't need her as much as she thought they did. The idea was sort of liberating. She'd been living on hold for so long it was nice to have a change in her life.

After Tuesday night's game that week, on the drive home Rick told her that his coach had announced an unscheduled tournament the coming weekend. The same one she and Sean would be out of town. Rick had already made arrangements to stay with a basketball buddy for the weekend, but she hated to miss the games. Still, she wouldn't let Sean down again. He deserved better. This time she would choose him over her brothers.

She'd never done anything like going away with a man before. Had never been straight up about where she would be when it came to her brothers. She had it bad. No, she was afraid she might be in love.

Where that was going to get her she had no idea. Did Sean feel the same way? It didn't matter; her heart was going to take a beating if he didn't feel the same.

After waiting impatiently for the coming weekend, Cynthia gazed out of the windshield as Sean pulled up the pine-lined drive to the side of the log cabin. A porch spanned the length of the front. The fading evening sun glistened orange off the lake nearby. There couldn't have been a more perfect spot in the world. She could hardly wait to have Sean to herself for a couple of days.

Together they climbed the steps to the porch. He unlocked the door and entered ahead of her as she looked off over the lake.

Cynthia joined him. "Sean, this is wonderful. I may never leave."

He flipped on a light over the sink. Coming to her, he pulled her into his arms. "That would suit me just fine. I'm not sure I could ever get enough of you." He kissed her.

Minutes later and leaving her panting for more of his kisses, he said, "I'd better get things in before it gets dark."

"I'll help." She started toward the door.

"No, you won't. This weekend is about me taking care of you. And you doing nothing that isn't just for you."

She followed him out on the porch. "Hey, when was that decided?"

"I did it on the way up here," he threw over his

shoulder. “Now hush and go explore the rest of the place. I’ll be done here soon.”

Cynthia did as he instructed. The main area was just one large room with the kitchen on one side and a sitting area with a fireplace on the other. She found two bedrooms at the back of the place. One was smaller with bunk beds and the other was larger with a bed that took up most of the space. A quilt covered it and there was another on the end of the bed. Outside the back door was an open-air shower.

“So what do you think?” Sean called.

“I love it.” She went back to the kitchen where he was unloading the bags of groceries they’d bought at a small store a few miles away.

“You hungry?” he asked.

“No. I’m still full from that burger. It was good.” They had stopped on the way at a local burger place his friend had recommended.

“I could tell from the amount of juice running down your chin.” He grinned at her then put a jug of milk in the refrigerator.

She raised her nose in the air. “Like you were any better.”

“What would you like to do first? We can walk

down to the lake. Sit on the porch. Or watch the rest of the sunset. Start a fire. It's up to you." Sean put the last of the supplies away.

"I think I would like to try out the interesting shower before it gets completely dark." She picked up her bag and carried it to the large bedroom. There she pulled out a new short nightgown and headed for the bath. She found what she needed before going outside. Hanging the towel on the rail, she turned on the water and made sure it was warm before she quickly undressed and stepped under the steaming water.

"I had no idea the shower was outside. I don't know about this," Sean said from the door opening above her.

"Come on in. This is rather liberating. Live a little, Doc."

Her face was lifted to the water when Sean stepped in behind her. His hands skimmed her hips, stomach and then cupped her breasts. "I've missed you to the point of pain," he said as he nuzzled at her ear. "The days were long and I can't wait to have you."

She turned and took him in her hand. "Doctor, I have just the cure for that."

* * *

Sean woke to Cynthia's body curled against his and his arm across her waist the next afternoon. They lay on the floor in front of the now cold fireplace.

To his great pleasure he'd woken this morning in bed with her tucked under him. The air had been crisp and he'd been warm and content. When was the last time he could have said that?

They'd had a late breakfast, then gone for a long walk along the edge of the lake. She'd dared him to go skinny-dipping. Laughing and shivering, they'd run back to the cabin for a hot shower. They'd then built a fire, and made love again. Now he hoped to do it all over again.

More than once she'd asked him if he was having fun. He was. A lot.

He'd never spent so much uninterrupted time with one woman and still wanted more of her. He wished he could have her in his life forever. Needed her was more accurate. He wasn't going to settle, nor let her, for one day here and another there. This weekend had proven he had to have her to keep him open to possibilities.

He was in love. There was no doubt about it.

How that had happened he had no idea. Maybe he did. It was simple: Cyn.

He looked down.

Cynthia was watching him. "Hey there, handsome."

Sean smiled. "Hey, beautiful."

They didn't even have a chance for a kiss before her phone rang. She looked away. "I'd better get that. Probably someone trying to sell me something but still. I told the boys not to call me unless it was an emergency." She untangled herself from him and went naked to pick up the phone.

He'd expected she might call home but to his joy she hadn't. Yet as a doctor, he knew the importance of people being able to get in contact so he accepted her need to answer.

"Hello."

"Yes. This is Cynthia Marcum."

"Oh, no."

Sean stood and came toward her.

"I'm on my way. Yes. I'm his sister. Next of kin."

This wasn't good. He moved closer.

"What hospital?" There was a pause. "UAB.

Good. I'm on my way. I'll be there in an hour and a half." She hung up. "We have to go." She started to the bedroom.

"What happened?" Sean followed her.

"Rick got pushed into the bleachers during the game. His face has been injured. He's going to need surgery."

Cynthia started dressing. She wouldn't even look at him.

"I'm sure he will be fine." He tried to take her into his arms but she pushed him away. "We need to go."

Sean didn't try further. No doubt she was letting guilt swamp her. As if she could have done anything if she had been there. Sean pulled on his clothes, threw his other items in his bag then called the hospital requesting to speak to the emergency department. After a few minutes, he had a clear picture of Rick's situation.

Cynthia joined him with her bag in hand.

"I just talked to the doctor seeing about Rick. He's going to be fine. He needs surgery but he's young and should do great." Sean hoped to reassure her. She was acting panicky. Her face twisted with worry, and her hands shaking.

"Do you know the man who's going to do it?" she asked.

"I do. It's me."

She searched his face. "You? Can he wait that long?"

"Cynthia, this isn't a life and death issue."

Her face turned furious. "He's my brother. As far as I'm concerned it is life or death!" Striding ahead of him, she was out of the door and almost to the car when she said, "I should have been there."

On the way to the hospital Cynthia said little. Her eyes were so serious and sad. Sean wanted to hold her but he couldn't do that while driving. He made a couple of calls and organized his team for the upcoming surgery. At the hospital, Sean pulled into his slot in the parking lot. Before he could turn off the engine, Cynthia was out of the car and stalking toward the ER. He caught up with her. "We'll go through the staff entrance."

At the nurses' station, he asked what trauma room Rick was in. When they entered she hurried to the bed.

"Oh, Rick, I'm sorry I wasn't there. How do

you feel?" She gently touched the top of his head, then his hand.

The boy did look awful with his swollen face and the purple and red discoloration beneath his eyes. Sean was used to the appearance but probably for Cyn it looked much worse on her beloved brother.

"Hey, Cyn. I'm fine. I'll be fine. It's just hard to breathe," Rick complained.

"I'm going to fix that," Sean said, stepping closer to the bed.

Rick looked at him with bloodshot watery eyes. "You're going to do the surgery?"

"You want the best nose guy in town, don't you?" Sean smiled at him.

"Yeah, I'd like to have a nose instead of a pancake."

"Understood." Sean touched Cynthia's back, gaining her attention. "I'm going to step out and look at the results from some tests I ordered. I'll be back to examine Rick in a few minutes." To Rick he said, "We'll be going into surgery within the hour."

Cynthia didn't even acknowledge him. Her actions baffled Sean. She was acting as if he'd caused Rick's accident. Was she blaming him for her not being there when Rick got hurt? Hadn't she learned from her parents that some things couldn't be prevented?

He reviewed all the material and discussed with the ER doctor what had been done so far for Rick, then returned to his room. Cynthia still stood beside his bed with her hand on his arm.

Sean stepped toward them. Cynthia threw him a quick glance when he announced, "Well, Rick, you took a good shot to the face. I've reviewed the X-rays and CT. You have an extreme septal hematoma. It'll need to be surgically repaired so you can breathe correctly. Thankfully you don't have a broken cheekbone. What I'll do is straighten your nose. You'll have packing inside and a brace across it when you come out of surgery. Give it a few weeks and you should be back to normal. Now, before I leave to get ready for surgery I need to give you a quick exam."

Cynthia stepped back and allowed him in closer to the bed. Sean gently touched around Rick's face, at his ears, jaw and neck. He finished, pleased that the young man didn't flinch any more than expected. Rick was lucky the injury wasn't worse.

There was a knock at the door. Ann Marie stuck her head in the room. She wore an unsure smile. "Can I come in?"

Rick groaned. "Now you get to see me as the Elephant Man."

Sean touched Cynthia's arm. "Can I talk to you outside for a minute?"

With an unsure look, she glanced back at Rick before following him out. Outside the room, she turned worried eyes up at Sean.

"I just wanted to give you an idea of what'll happen. Surgery will take a few hours at least. Rick will probably be out of it until morning. I'm going to give him some pretty strong pain meds. I want him to spend the night here just to make sure everything is okay and rule out a concussion. He had a major trauma to his head. If he has no issues he should be able to go home tomorrow."

"Is he going to be okay?" Her eyes begged for reassurance.

Sean hugged her and kissed the top of her head. "Rick's going to be fine. Promise." He released her so he could look at her face. "You can stay here with him until he's ready to go to surgery. I've instructed one of the nurses to show you to the waiting room. I'll meet you there when we're done."

She grabbed his arm. "Take care of my brother." "You know I will." Sean patted her hand and headed down the hall.

Cynthia didn't like waiting. Especially when a loved one was involved. She'd paced the waiting room, spoken to Mark who was at work and would be here as soon as he got off. Now she was mindlessly watching the TV without really hearing or seeing it. Other families had come and gone in the waiting room, but she remained.

She took a chair and put her head in her hands. What had she been doing? She should have been at the basketball game instead of off with Sean. She was responsible for Rick. When he had needed her she'd been curled in Sean's arms. Her parents would be so disappointed in her.

Cynthia hated it but she was going to have to give up Sean. There was no way she could meet her obligations to her brothers and to Sean too. One of them would have to wait. Unfortunately, right now in her life that must be Sean. She would be tearing her heart out to do it but she would. It wasn't fair to him to take second seat all the time. If she gave him up it wouldn't be that way any more.

She must to tell him soon. For his sake and hers.

With relief, and a sadness that went bone deep, she was glad to see Sean come through the doors toward her. He was still wearing his blue surgical cap and matching scrubs. What she appreciated the most was the smile on his face. Surgery had been successful.

When she reached him, he pulled her close. She resisted holding tight. He gave her a concerned look. She didn't give him time to ask questions. "By the look on your face Rick is doing well."

"He is. He's being moved to a room and you should be able to see him in about an hour. Someone will come tell you what room. They were having to juggle rooms when I last asked. Are you good?" Sean studied her. Anxiety showing in his eyes.

"I'm fine now."

"Good. I hate to leave you again but I have some paperwork to do. I'll see you later in Rick's room."

She nodded. "Thanks for taking care of my brother."

He smiled and brushed her cheek with a finger. "Anything for you."

That statement didn't make her feel any better about what she had to do.

Two hours later Cynthia was sitting at Rick's bedside when Sean entered. He'd changed back into the shirt and jeans he'd worn to the hospital.

"How's the patient doing?" He studied Rick.

She looked at her brother. "Okay, I think. He moans every once in a while, but that's it."

"He'll have a lot of swelling but it'll be gone in a couple of weeks. In about six weeks you shouldn't be able to tell this even happened." Sean sounded pleased with his work.

"Thanks," she murmured.

"Not a problem. Just sorry this happened to him." Sean came around the bed to her.

"How about going home with me and getting

some rest? I can bring you back first thing in the morning."

Cynthia didn't stand to meet him. She wasn't going anywhere until Rick did. "I'm going to stay here tonight."

"You don't need to do that. We have a great nursing staff."

She shook her head.

Giving her a curious look, Sean pulled the other chair in the room over beside her and sat. "We can stay awhile longer, then I think you need to go home."

"Don't tell me what I should do," she snapped. "I can take care of myself."

Sean sat straight, studying her. "What's going on, Cynthia?"

"We need to talk." She finally looked him in the eyes but wished she hadn't. Those beautiful blue eyes she would miss.

"That doesn't sound good."

Clutching her hands in her lap, she whispered, "This isn't going to work."

"What?" He looked at Rick as if he might have done something wrong.

"Us," she said.

He scoffed. "It seemed to be working great this morning."

"I can't do it. It's not fair to you. I should've been there when Rick got hurt."

"You have to be kidding! What would have happened differently if you had been?"

Cynthia leaned toward him keeping her voice low. She wanted him to understand so badly. "I don't know but I have a responsibility to my brothers. Right now in my life they come first. That isn't fair to you. I care about you too much to do that to you."

Sean quietly said an expletive. "No, you don't, or you wouldn't do this." With a jerk he stood, forced her to her feet and led her out of the door. "We don't need to disturb Rick. Come with me." When she hesitated, he said, "A nurse will be in to check on him."

They walked to the end of the hall to where there was an empty room. Sean closed the door firmly behind them after they entered.

He faced her. "We have something good between us. Real. And you want to throw it away because you feel guilty or irresponsible, or some other ridiculous emotion because you weren't at the game when your brother got hurt. You're his sister. Not his parent. And if you haven't noticed, he's of age. Mark is as well. They're no longer your baby brothers. They are men! They're old enough to take care of themselves. You need to let go. For their sakes as well as yours."

She cringed. That might be true but it didn't mean they didn't need her. "Like you did with your family. They didn't measure up to what you thought they should be so when you got old enough you dumped them completely."

"You don't know anything about my family and me," he snarled softly.

"Sure I do." Cynthia took a step toward him. "They chose everything over you. Leaving you with no security. When you could get away you made sure that was never an issue for you again. To the point you had no idea how to have fun. You made sure that you went into a field you are talented in, but also had a good income. Yet you never spend money on anything other than necessities because you live daily in fear of being like your parents. You're afraid to really live or experience life. Other than this weekend, when was the last time you got away? Lived a little? Laughed?"

He glared at her.

"That's right." She made herself continue. "You haven't because you don't know how to let go. You don't even see that you need that in your life. I understand your parents are a little… uh…unconventional, but I would bet they would say they are happy. Are you happy, Sean?

"I'd also bet anything you've smiled more and laughed more since you met my family than you have in years. We need people around us regardless of whether or not they fit within the lines we want them to. I learned the hard way that life is about people. Not about how much money we have but memories. Creating them is what matters. It's all we have when they're gone. Security comes from the ones we love, not from a bank account."

Sean flinched as if she'd slapped him. He recovered and took a step toward her. "Yeah, but we also need to break away from our family so that we can live our own lives," he bit out. "Become individuals. Your brothers, your family unit is so important to you that you don't think beyond them. There isn't room for anyone else. You could go back to school if you want to, or be with me, but you use your brothers to hide behind. What is it you're afraid of? That someone will let you down again? Don't put that on me." He pointed to the floor with his index finger. "I'm here. I was there last night. I'll be there tomorrow if you let me.

"You might be right about me needing too much financial security. But I've never had someone I wanted to spend money on before. Until now. My family is a complicated issue. Not one I think you can understand because your parents weren't like mine. Yet with all our differences I find that you're the only woman for me." He glared at her. "I love you."

Cynthia looked at him in disbelief. Her chest tightened. He loved her. She wanted to run to him and wrap her arms around him but she couldn't. Though they stood so close they were so far apart when it came to how they lived their lives, what they believed.

"Yeah, you heard that right. I love you. But I won't accept you not being all that you can and want to be. It's not healthy not to move on. You have done the job your parents wanted you to. Your brothers are great. Even Mark will find his way. But he must do it for himself, just like you must. Your welfare will always be my first consideration. I'd love to see you become that nurse you dream of being. With your large capacity for caring you would be nothing but great at it. I bet your mom and dad didn't want you to stop living just because they did."

Cynthia sucked in a breath. That statement hurt.

He paused for a second then said, "Don't be afraid to take the opportunity to live again. You might find out I'm more fun than you think I am."

"I just can't right now," she said softly. "I have responsib—"

"I'm sorry to hear that. You think about it, Cyn. You know where I am if you ever move beyond the past and want to create a future."

CHAPTER TEN

DAYS LATER SEAN still couldn't accept the way Cynthia had reacted when Rick was injured. She'd implied he'd somehow been responsible for it. She couldn't see she'd moved into a holding pattern when her parents had died and couldn't or wouldn't find her way out of it. He cared for her too much not to help her face reality.

The day after their fight he'd made rounds and released Rick to go home. She'd not been in her brother's room when he'd come in to see him. Sean suspected that Cynthia had asked the nurse what time he usually made rounds and made sure she was gone for breakfast at that time. She was dodging him.

A few days later he returned to the cabin to get the things they had left behind. It was a painful trip. Everywhere he looked there was Cynthia laughing or smiling at him. They had been cheated. He wanted that time back.

He'd known unhappiness but losing Cynthia was misery. Nothing in his life seemed right. Everything was the same. He was seeing patients, doing surgery, and going home to an empty house, yet his whole world was out of line. The nights were the worst. He'd taken to sleeping in his chair because he couldn't stand being in his bed without her. Even taking a shower brought back bittersweet memories.

Sean had worked to order his adult life, to live with stability and security. Now a small, outspoken, passionate, big-hearted woman had shaken the foundation. One he desperately wanted back in his life. But that was her choice. So far he'd seen no indication she was going to change her mind.

Cynthia was still doing his transcription. When he requested a report, there were her initials on the bottom next to his. As the old saying went: So close yet so far away. Just as they had been standing in that hospital room when they'd argued. He looked daily, despite his best efforts not to, for an email from her. Each day he was disappointed.

His disposition had become so poor that his

office manager suggested that candy and flowers almost always covered any sins.

Sean wasn't sure that her pun had been intentional but it had hit home. But what could he do? What choices did he have? He'd left the door open. Cynthia hadn't come through it.

When Rick came for his follow-up visit at Sean's office he'd hoped Cynthia would be with him, only to be relieved when she wasn't. It would have killed him to watch her walk away again. Rick didn't ask him any questions about his and Cynthia's breakup, but when he left he said, "I hope I see you around."

Sean responded, "I'd like that too."

He thought Cynthia gave her family priority too often but she had said things about his relationship with his family that had him thinking. Being around her and her brothers, he'd remembered things about his family life he'd chosen not to examine in a long time. His parents had loved him the best way they knew how. But even with their haphazard lifestyle there had been laughter around the dinner table. They'd had game nights. His efforts at school had been praised and posted on the bulletin board in the kitchen. Life hadn't been all bad. There had been fun then.

Could he have been so narrow-minded he'd been unfair to his parents? Had he expected perfection? Hadn't they been a significant part of making him who he was today? Would he be as driven as a doctor or have worked so hard on the new procedure if it wasn't for his upbringing? Maybe it was time to reach out to his parents and say thank you.

At home that evening Sean picked up his phone and looked at the number for the second time. What if they didn't have time for him? Or wanted him to join in another one of their businesses? What if they didn't care if they saw him? He punched the number.

It rang three times before the voice of his mother said, "Hello."

"Hi, Mom."

"Sean, is that you? Oh, honey, how're you? It's been so long. We've missed you so much."

The sick feeling in Sean's middle turned to one of joy. After the way he'd treated them in the last few years he wouldn't have been surprised if she had hung up on him.

"Mom, how're you doing?"

"We're well. Lisa and Bill are too. Are you okay?" Her voice sounded concerned.

"I'm fine." He was heartbroken but he wouldn't go into that now. That wasn't what this call was about. Yet Cynthia had been behind him making it. "I was wondering if I could come visit sometime soon."

"You're welcome any time." Hope filled her voice.

"Would this weekend be okay?" Sean would deserve it if they said no.

"Sure, honey."

"Then I'll see you Saturday afternoon. Around four," Sean told her.

His mother sounded sincere when she said, "Your daddy and I can hardly wait."

A few days later, Sean pulled into his parents' drive. He hadn't climbed out of his car before his mother and father were there to greet him. It reminded him of how eager he'd been to see Cynthia drive up at his house for the first time. Pure delight to see her had driven his actions. Did his parents feel the same way about seeing him?

His mother hugged him so tightly she almost

took his breath. His father patted him on the shoulder at the same time. When his mother released him, she had tears in her eyes. His father shook his hand and pulled him into a hug for a second.

"Come in. Lisa and Bill are here with their kids," his mother said as she herded them toward the house.

He and his father followed more slowly. "It's good to have you home, Sean. Your mother will be walking on air for weeks after this visit."

Guilt washed over Sean for staying away so long.

Lisa and Bill were equally glad to see him. The family had a talkative dinner with memories and laughter shared. The only time it became uncomfortable was when his father mentioned a new internet deal he was working on. Sean cringed.

"Let's not talk business at the dinner table," his mom quickly said.

His father moved on to another subject.

Some things never changed. The difference was that Sean was his own man now. He could live his life the way he wanted to.

To his amazement his brother and sister and their partners had solid jobs. They had seemed to go along with their parents' ideas when they had been younger. After dinner, he and Bill went to the den.

"I'm glad you came. We don't see enough of you," Bill said as he took a chair opposite the TV.

Sean took the other. "I should have done better, I know."

"Putting up with Mom and Dad always going after a great deal was hard on you. Not having enough money. Lisa and I were older and took it better, but you were embarrassed. You wanted to play sports and do things we didn't care anything about. I'm not surprised you've stayed away."

Sean had had no idea Bill had noticed how he had felt. "I've done all right. It took me a while to realize that the way I was brought up might have motivated me."

Bill nodded. "I hear you have made a name for yourself in Birmingham."

"I'm proud of my work. It's very satisfying to help people." Sean only wished his personal life were the same. Was it too late to find happiness with Cynthia? Apparently, she didn't want him. She hadn't contacted him. He looked for an email every day. His phone remained nearby all the time. She hadn't said anything about loving him. Maybe she didn't.

His father joined them, taking a seat on the couch. "You'll stay with us tonight, won't you, Sean?"

Sean smiled. He and his parents would probably never agree but despite their differences they still loved him. He loved them too. "That sounds nice, Dad."

Cynthia still saved Sean's dictation tapes for last but now it was because it broke her heart to hear his voice when she couldn't touch him or be loved by him. The days had turned into long and painful weeks. Still, she knew she had done the right thing. He deserved better. She couldn't be what he needed right now. When she could be would he still want her?

For so long she had dreamed of him. Built him up in her mind. He was almost too good to be true then, but now she knew him as a man with foibles and issues, which made her love him more. Sean was perfect for her. No one would ever replace him. He was the love of her life. But she couldn't tell him that.

She'd spent the first week they had been apart taking care of Rick. He'd been recovering so well he'd got aggravated with her. It was as if he were pushing her away so he could handle his own life. He had gone to his follow-up visit with Sean without her. She wasn't sure she could have gone anyway but she was relieved when Rick had insisted he could do it himself.

Mark seemed happier than ever now that he was working and no longer going to college. She still hoped he would return but for now learning the value of being a good employee might be worthwhile.

His car had been declared dead so they were down to two cars. Instead of throwing a fit and demanding she make all the concessions, he and Rick had worked out sharing Rick's car, only using hers when it was convenient with her. Mark had matured and she hadn't even realized it.

Why hadn't she noticed how responsible her

brothers had become? Had Sean been right? Was she refusing to admit that they didn't need her as they once had? Maybe she needed them to need her more than they really did. *Had* she been hiding behind them so she wouldn't have to move on with her life? Was she postponing her dreams out of fear? Had she pushed Sean away because of that as well?

When Mark and Rick had asked what had happened between her and Sean she'd said, "We just didn't work out."

They'd given her skeptical looks but said no more.

The weeks had crawled by and still Sean filled her thoughts during the day and dreams at night. The tears were the worst. There was no telling when they would flow. She was miserable and didn't know how to change her state. Her plan was to endure until the pain eased.

Two months after she and Sean had broken up, she asked Rick during family dinner night, "When do you need to sign up for class?"

"I don't have to do that for a few more weeks," Rick said, digging into his potatoes. "I've got this."

"I just don't want you to miss that date."

Rick put down his fork. "I know what I need to do. You don't have to tell me everything. I'm grown. I can take care of it. If I don't that's my problem."

"Uh, Rick and I've been talking," Mark said. "We think it's time for you to stop treating us like your children and start acting more like our sister. We don't want to be told what to do all the time."

Could a stab in the heart hurt as much? She looked from one to the other. "Really? I didn't know I was doing that. I thought I was helping you."

"You do. But it's time to stop," Rick volunteered quietly.

"We're tired of it. I'm working and Rick's finishing high school in a few weeks and going to college. It's time for you to stop worrying about us all the time."

What had brought this on? They'd always gone along with what she said until recently. "How long have you felt this way?"

"A long time," Mark said.

Rick nodded.

Mark gave her a direct look. "We wanted us to stay together after Mom and Dad died just as much as you. We wanted to make you happy. But we couldn't move anything in the house. You wanted to keep on having family dinner night because Mom did it. All the calls at nine. At first it worked but it still wasn't the same because they weren't here. We think it's time for all of us to have our own lives. Even you."

"We—" Mark nodded toward Rick "—appreciate all you have done for us. Giving up school and working all the time. And being there for us. We want to make our own decisions now. Find our own ways. You should too."

"I had no idea you felt this way." Or had she just not been listening?

Rick said, "Now you do. Hey, we could be college students together. How cool would that be?"

"I think that would be nice." She smiled. It would be wonderful if she could go back to school. Get that nursing degree? "Okay, I'll make a deal with you. If you help me more around here, then I'll consider going back to school. You have to also promise to tell me when I'm being too bossy and I'll promise to stop."

"I don't know if I can agree to the first but I can sure tell you when you're being too bossy," Rick said.

They all laughed.

"What we really think you should do is use the money that Mom and Dad left us that we know you've been saving, to get a place of your own. If you stay here, you'll always be thinking about us. Buy a condo or a house of your own. Rick and I can live here. Or we could be the ones to move out."

Cynthia's heart tightened. They didn't want her around any more?

"I see that look on your face," Mark said. "We're not trying to get rid of you per se. We need some space and we think you do too. We can still get together for dinner once a week."

It sounded as if her brothers had already moved on. She was the one stuck in the past. Where had she heard that before? Sean had seen something she hadn't been able to see.

"Hey, Cyn," Rick said. "You deserve to have some fun too."

It would be tough but she would do what was necessary to make them all happy. Her brothers seemed to have their lives together. It was time she did the same with her own. "I love you guys." She opened her arms wide. "Group hug."

A week later Cynthia slipped the last tape on her list into the machine. Her middle tightened at knowing what she would hear next. There was no way she could heal if she continued to listen to Sean's deep voice regularly so she'd given her notice to his office manager. She could use the money, especially after she'd decided to return to school, but working for Sean wasn't helping her to move on.

But was she doing that? Their issues had stemmed from her inability to let go. Now she was trying to make that change. More than once Mark and Rick had given her a look when she'd said something and she'd been able to catch herself a few times before she did.

She'd already made a step in that direction by enrolling in school. As happy as that would make her, something would always be missing. Sean. She wanted him back in her life in a bigger way than just listening to his voice. All of him was what she needed, wanted.

He'd told her the door was open when or if she got ready to talk. She knew full well how to get in touch with him. But he'd not tried to approach her in all these weeks. He'd said he loved her. Had she hurt him so badly that he wanted nothing to do with her? He'd accepted her decision without even trying to contact her once. Maybe he had moved on to another woman. The thought made her sick. She'd found happiness but her blinding devotion to her brothers had lost her the man she loved.

If she did contact Sean could he forgive her for being such an idiot?

She could continue living as she had for the last couple of months, depressed and lonely, or she could try to do something about it. How could she lose? She would finish his dictation and then compose an email. Try to see if that door was still open.

Pushing the button, she opened Sean's dictation. "Hey, Cyn. I hope you're well. I wanted to let you know I received the grant."

Her chest tightened. Moisture filled her eyes. It was the first time Sean had said anything personal during his dictation. It was so little yet so much. Cynthia pushed another button and ran the report back to listen again. Was there a hopeful note in his voice? Had this been his way of reminding her he still cared? She listened once again. Whatever the reason, she was seizing the opportunity and going for it. She was moving forward, grasping what she wanted.

The transcription could wait. She had an email to write.

Hi Sean
I'm well. I'm glad to hear about the grant.
I owe you an apology. Could we talk sometime?
Cyn

The one thing they'd always shared was honesty. If he'd changed his mind about her or found someone else then so be it, but at least she had made a step forward. There would be no regrets. This wasn't a game. Her heart was at stake.

Before she could change her mind, with a shaking hand she pushed send.

Sean turned on his computer for the first time after his last patient left. As he glanced at it one email stood out. For a second he just stared at it.

He'd taken a chance, couldn't help himself when he'd spoken to Cynthia directly in his dictation. Somehow he wanted her to know he was still there, caring about her. He wasn't sure how she would react.

What if she still didn't want to have anything to do with him? They'd said some harsh words to each other that day in the hospital. She might still be mad and tell him to leave her alone. He'd read the note from his office manager that Cynthia was no longer going to work for him. Was she cutting all ties?

There was no way for him to know until he opened her email. With fear gnawing at him like a wild animal, he clicked on her note. He quickly read it. Then read it again. There was nothing there to think what she might say would be any more than a business discussion between employee and employer. Yet that was at least something compared to no contact over the last few months.

Sean checked the time. It was late to ask if he could meet her but he couldn't wait. Excitement pushed the fear away. At least she was willing to see him. He wouldn't let this chance pass him by.

It's great to hear from you, Cyn.
I know it's late, but would you like to meet me somewhere? A restaurant, maybe?
Sean

Seconds later an email dropped into his box.

I would, but I don't have a car tonight. I hate to inconvenience you, but could you come to my house?

He quickly replied.

I'll be there in an hour.

There was just enough time to stop by his place and one more. Finally he had hopes his life would be back to normal. That was, with Cynthia in it.

Cynthia nervously paced the porch watching for Sean's car to come up the street. She had no idea what would happen between them. What she wished for was a whole other thing.

Her eyes widened when a late-model luxury car pulled into the drive. Who else was coming to her house? She was shocked to see Sean step out of it. Her heart was in her throat. Would he forgive her?

He looked at her expectantly, as if he was unsure of his reception. “Hi.”

She did love his voice. In fact, she loved all of him. No one could look more wonderful. It was all she could do not to run to him. If she did would his arms open wide? She settled for a simple, “Hey.”

Reaching back into the car, he brought out a spray of spring flowers and a box.

Who was this person in front of her?

Sean came up the walk. When he reached her he just stood there looking at her. She did the same. He pulled at everything in her. She wanted to touch him so badly she pushed her hands into the pockets of her knit dress to stop herself. “I, uh, like your new car.” That seemed like a safe place to start.

“Thanks. I just got it the other day. I decided after I visited my parents that I needed to make some changes. Loosen up a little bit.”

“You did?” She was so glad to hear he’d been to see them.

“I did.”

"So how're your parents?" More than that, she wanted to know how he was doing after seeing them.

He shrugged. "They're the same. But, they're my parents. I don't have to like how they run their lives but I can still love them."

She nodded. "That's true. Come on in, or we could sit out here." She pointed toward the porch swing.

"I'm good out here if you don't think you'll be too cool?" He seemed hesitant to enter the house. What could he be afraid of? She was the one who'd messed up.

"I'm okay." Her body was so heated by having him close she felt she'd never get cold again. She took a seat on the swing. He didn't join her.

"These are for you." He handed her the flowers and the box of candy. "They're a thank-you for helping with the grant. You were the first person I wanted to tell."

She accepted the gifts. "Thank you. The flowers are beautiful and I love chocolate."

He shifted from one foot to the other. Was Sean nervous? "My office manager says they cover most ills."

Had he talked to his office manager about her? He was such a private person she couldn't imagine what that conversation had been like. "They're a good starter. I'm so glad you got the grant. You deserved it."

"I was happy."

"You should be." They were talking but not really saying anything. Taking a deep breath, she said, "I appreciate you coming over. I owe you an apology for the way I acted when Rick was hurt. You were wonderful and I treated you horribly. More importantly you were right about me and how I was treating my brothers. They're men and I have to let go. I've started to do so.

"In fact, I've signed up for school. I'll have to repeat a semester but if I pass my test I should enter nursing school in the fall."

"Now I'm the one proud of you." Sean looked genuinely pleased.

She had no doubt from his tone that he was. He had always encouraged and supported her. "I'm sorry I was so hard on you."

Sean sat down beside her, turned to her. "I wasn't much better. I was so caught up in trying to not be like my parents I had gone completely in the opposite direction. They made me who I am. For that I should be grateful. I'm trying to lighten up some."

Cynthia looked at the gifts in her hands. He had certainly let go to buy something so frivolous. "So that's where these—" she indicated the flowers and candy "—and the car come in?"

He shrugged. "Yeah. But I leased the car." He gave her a boyish grin. "I couldn't let go completely."

She laughed and placed her gifts in the corner of the swing. "I'm glad you haven't changed altogether. I liked the old Sean."

He looked at her closely. "Could you still like him even with the modifications?"

Her heart picked up a beat. What was he asking? "Yes."

Sean took her fingers. "Enough to start over and give him another chance?"

Cynthia removed her hand from his and stood. His face dropped. He started to stand but she moved in front of him. Putting her hand on his shoulder, she nudged him back and stood between his legs. Sean watched her intently. He looked unsure and curious at the same time.

"I don't want to start over." Sean started to move but Cynthia continued, "I want what we've already had, then more. I want forever."

Sean had feared for a second that Cynthia was going to reject him. He looked at her in disbelief, then he grabbed her and pulled her to him. His lips found hers and she wrapped her arms around his neck and held on as if she would never let him go. This was what had been missing in his life. She was his life.

He pulled back. "I meant it when I said I loved you. You are my rock, my security."

She cupped his face. "I sure hope so because I love you too. You're the most important person to me. I won't ever let you forget it." She kissed him with all the love she had in her heart. Minutes later she pulled away. "By the way, I forgot to tell you that I'm going to be homeless soon."

Sean pulled her into his lap, his brows going together as he looked at her.

She smiled at him. "My brothers told me in no uncertain terms it was time for me to find my own place or they would."

He chuckled. "Maybe I can help you with that

problem. Would you marry me and share mine? We could have fun together for the rest of our lives."

"Nothing could sound nicer or more perfect." She kissed him.

Sean pulled back and searched her face. "Was that a yes?"

"It's most definitely a yes!"

* * * * *

If you enjoyed this story, check out these other great reads from Susan Carlisle:

THE SURGEON'S CINDERELLA
THE DOCTOR'S SLEIGH BELL PROPOSAL
WHITE WEDDING FOR A SOUTHERN BELLE
MARRIED FOR THE BOSS'S BABY

All available now!

Psst!